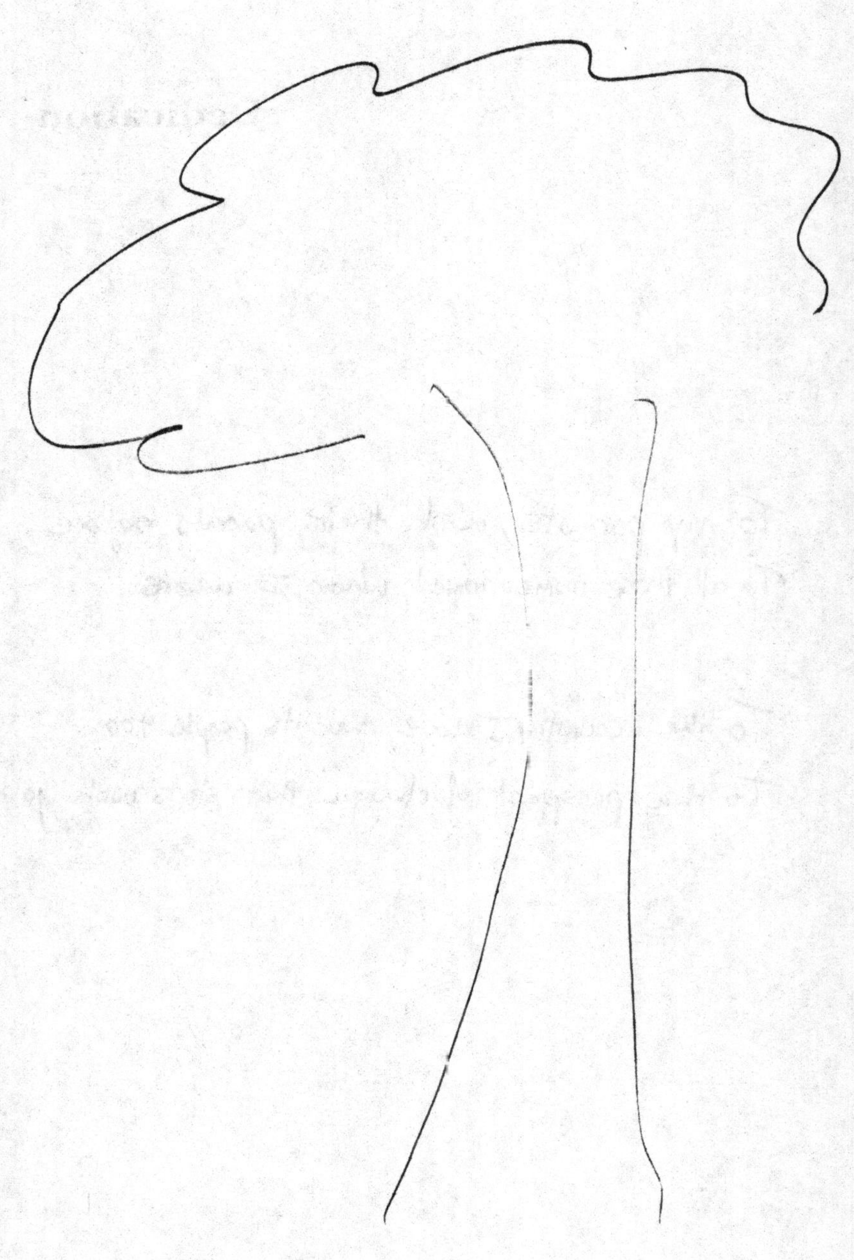

Dedication

To my parents, and their parents before
To all those unmentioned, whom I adore.

To the country I love, and its people too
To the prospect of change, that starts with you.

Acknowledgements

For a relatively short novel it has taken me a tremendous amount of time and energy to complete. I am thankful to finally be able to share this message with you all and thank you for joining me on this journey. Even now I still see potential for growth within the story but feel it necessary to now open it up to you, the dear reader.

There is little merit in the claim that I was able to complete this project alone. It took me much longer than I thought, and I needed to lean on the people around me for support during the process. Without them I would not have had the strength to complete this work; nor be as inspired as I am for the future works to come. Over the past years I have been privileged with the trust of some amazing people that inspired themes within this story — for which I am forever grateful.

It is with a heavy heart that one of my closest companions along this journey has since passed, Phillip Dempsey Narkle was a humble man of intense passion for sharing culture and an incredibly gifted artist. I was privileged to regularly visit with him over the last five years and will cherish his memory for the rest of my life.

It is with great appreciation that I recognise the

contribution of the Noongar people and those who have opened their hearts to me and accepted me into their grace. I am forever grateful for your kindess. I thank these people for accepting me into their hearts and sharing with me their experiences and offering further direction towards the successful completion of this project.

Robert Innes
Phil Narkle
George Innes
Dennis 'Noongali' Kickett
Amanda Gay
Rochelle Stacey
Kayla Holt
Marina Humphreys

Kerry Seaby
Lukas Best
Professor. Marion Kickett
Mark Patrick.
Elaine Innes
Charmaine Holt
Amelia Wilkinson
Cassidy Weinman
Kim Williams

Kickstarter Campaign

I have been able to fund this initial print through some very generous people. I'd like to thank Rob and Jess Hales, Ronald Liu, Brenton Lush, Ishka McNulty, Neven Mackowiecki, Louise Youens, Alison Dalziel, Jess Karlsson, Murray Trueman, Kayla Stock, Elizabeth Eidenschink, Eric Schaefer [First Backer], and 'Sophia' for their contributions towards making this project a reality.

I would like to give an extended sentiment of my appreciation to the follow list of people who have been instrumental in the completion of this work. Without them I am confident that it would still be an intimidating word document locked deep in my desktop. Thank you for believing in me and this project when it was still budding into maturity. Your support will be forever remembered with all the fondness my heart is capable.

The Beaufort Rotary Club
Joseph Gay
Chris Tann + Jenny Jigoor
Michael + Monica Gay

George + Mary Innes
Andrew Woods
Allan + Joyce Martin
Lukas + Josie Best

Introduction

The terra nullius declaration of Australia is perhaps
the most damaging document in human history. It
successfully collectivised and dehumanised hundreds
of unique cultural mythologies, languages, spiritu-
alities and societal practices. This pan-Aboriginal-
ity continues to linger in the systemic institutions of
Australia, and it is up to us all - as active citizens - to
correct this injustice. After the terrible floods that
ravaged Queensland in the early months of 2011,
in an environment of chaos and destruction, it fell
to the people to clean up the situation. Rather than
arguing: 'Well, why should I clean up? I didn't cause
this mess!' or surrendering to the magnitude of the
task before beginning *or* coming to a stand-still in
discussions about how we should approach the disaster – people got to work. People united and did what
needed to be done. It was, and always will be, up to
people to effect change.

When I began my Ph.D in 2014 I was frustrated
at the prospect of producing a dusty bound disser-
tation that would remain on the shelves of a univer-
sity library – read by a whole three people. I wanted
something more from the project. I wanted to start
conversations; with co-workers, with family and
friends, and in government offices. And so here we

are now with a completed narrative that encapsulates the concepts for our collective investigation. Additionally, I am donating a portion of every book sold directly back into the community through not-for-profit organisations in an effort to stimulate real change at a local level.

Story is a key element of breaking down perception and exploring unconscious bias. It is essential to let people discover a message for themselves, through points of relation such as identifying with the experiences of a character through empathy; rather than being talked at in a lecture on the same message. Story is also key to easing the population along the journey of historical acceptance and the accountability of citizenship for the future. It is up to all of us to act against the inequalities that still exist, on all levels of society, between Indigenous and non-Indigenous Australians. My response is 'Under the Shade', because if we can start to create a new platform from which to view the world, we may finally begin to deconstruct the ill-informed one from which once we stood.

I wholeheartedly welcome criticism, feedback and discussion. Please write to — *info@undertheshade.com.au* — I will endeavour to address all inquiries. I recognise that I am by no means a full bottle on any subject and that I always have potential to develop my understandings.

People are the power and when we are united, we're unstoppable. The politicians that administer this country are representatives elected to public service, yet that fact feels forgotten in recent years. We continue to elect campaigners – not effective people of action. If we want something done in this country, it is upon us all to act. As we have seen with the horrific response around the most recent bushfires – both preventative and reactive – of this Federal Government, the 'bottom-line' is held with higher regard than human equity and empathy. Only now that the flood of social support is coming in do we breathe an air of relief; an air already clouded with the smug fog of political campaigning.

Let us remind ourselves that we are the power. And that when we are divided the institutions capitalise on your disunity and bickering. Instead we must unite in our difference and our country will blossom out of its adolescence into the enlightened new world.

Enjoy.

Contents

Mythology

This short list can aid in the understanding of the literary universe.

WULGI – The Wulgi are beings that exist in a dimension between Walken and the main character of the narrative. They are the spirits of passed Kadachi and serve as the watchers of time.

WALKEN – Walken is the creation being of the story. She is a being of intense white light, surrounded by seven companions of coloured light– known as the wisps - and can travel through all things that are natural but powerless to elements outside her world.

WISPS – The wisps, **MIRDA, WOOYAN, YOORDA, YOONT, NODJAM, VIOLA,** and **KAWA** orbit Walken's white core as a helix. They aid and assist Walken.

KADACHI – The kah-dah-chi are the spiritual guides for each community. Their roles allow them to communicate directly with the spirit world and communicate back to the people of their community.

SONGLINES – Song lines have been used for thousands of years to help navigate country, and when song lines are 'sung' the melody of the song reflects the nature of the land it is describing. Song lines provide signs, cues and important knowledge about the past, present and future, and trace the journeys of ancestral spirits during creation times.

Story Breaks

These symbols are designed to make the transition between stories easier. There's no need to memorise them, it'll quickly make sense as the story goes on.

A break in story in the same arc.

A break in the spiritual story arc.

A change in time within the physical story arc.

A change of story arch between the physical and spiritual.

CHAPTER 1

"Ok, ok. I think I've got it. Where are we again?" asked Dom.

"We're in both the happened, and the happening," replied Kenny.

"Yes… of course. Now. How does that work, exactly?" said Dom.

"Like a dreaming when you sleep. One moment, you're you. Then you're on your way through an adventure. It may be treacherous anticipation or bring you joy from past memory. One must have happened after the other, but they are also both happening at the same time. It's the same here. It's been the same here since the very beginning."

There was once and still is, both now and then—and all time to come—a place to inhabit time. An observation deck of sorts. From here you can see anything: from where the dinosaurs roam to the polyphonic telephone. There are only a few beings that remain in this place beyond time and they can often see fit to intervene in their entertainment.

They were a thin frame of flesh strapped taut to a bony core. Heavy brown cloaks draped over them and dragged on the ground behind them as they walked. Each of the Wulgi's eyes glowed through the dark shroud of the large baggy hoods they wore over their heads. Their eyes—deep red, yellow, green and blue—appeared to hover in the pitch black darkness of the frontside of their cowls.

"Oh! Here's one! Look over there," said Koko, peering into the infinite horizon. The group moved to it in a flash.

"Look how cramped they are! It must smell horrible in there," said Kojak.

It was a boardroom filled with stressed and tired people. Their skin perspired under their triple-layered suits. Beads rolled down their foreheads, greeting the air conditioner that was on full. The Wulgi placed themselves, disguised, within the boardroom. They transformed themselves to blend into their new space. Two were now flies, one chose to be a pot plant over in the corner, and the other, a water cooler—all out of cups.

"Before I begin, I have to acknowledge the people who are the traditional custodians of this land where this meeting takes place and extend the same respect to them both past and present," said the stuffy man bulging through the buttons of his jacket.

"**What did he say?**" asked Kenny, a fly on the wall, telepathically to his party.

"**He said he acknowledged the past,**" replied Kojak.

"**Well... what's the alternative? It's not like it didn't happen,**" Kenny replied, pointing to the west.

"**Are we having custard?**" asked Dom excitedly as bubbles popped up from the depths of his refrigerated stomach.

"**The Fatman said 'custodian'. Now quiet down, I want to hear the rest,**" commanded Koko.

The room was still for a moment in anticipation.

"We are being met with resistance, sir," explained another suited mannequin seated on the long side of the important table. "The people there, they are not prepared to move. Our agents have tried in vain to negotiate terms; however, they are yet to adequately represent what it is they're after. We've offered capital to the sum of the land's current value—not that a dust bowl warrants much finance. The bottom line is that, if they're unable to use the land for sustainable growth, we will have to relocate the community to a place of utility to the government. Somewhere more suitable, Mr Chairman. There comes a point where they're just being unreasonable."

"He must sit a lot," said Dom.

"Sit a lot?" said Kojak.

"The Chairman. He must sit down a lot. He even looks like a chair. That's why they call him the Chair-man... I want you all to call me the clever man—cause I'm always one step ahead of you lot," boasted Dom.

Kenny and Koko—the flies, looked at one another from their perches.

"Ok, clever man," they said sarcastically.

"Good. Good. And what's our progress with legal?" continued the Chairman, sweeping his thin grey hair from his brow. His breathing was heavy through his mouth, which gaped open below a moustache of beaded sweat.

"Well, sir," piped up another suckling drone from the long side of the table, "the term 'unsustainable' is a bit of a stretch when applying it to this instance. These isolated communities are actually within our budget to maintain; therefore, the problem becomes a bit more complicated."

"That is the nature of war," replied the Chairman. "A series of moves and counter moves. They're damned clever, you know!" He thought for a moment. His hands, linked by his index fingers, extended and rested on his wide philtrum. "It's a battle, you see. Always a battle. Just have to out think 'em. Are these communities able to contribute to the wider collective of our state?"

His lackeys shuffled through their papers in search of a response. The room filled with anxious competition. The papers fanned the foul sweat around the room.

"Nn-no, sir. They have a small production industry, but only small crafted items—mainly to keep them busy. The revenue from these ventures is insignificant."

"This deal is far too important to our state. It cannot be stalled any longer over semantics. So, here's what we'll—" The Chairman broke off, coughing in a suffocating fit. After regaining his composure with a sip of water, he continued. "First, close the shops. We'll send in food rations monthly via our controlled non-government organisations, then start restrictions. Then, close the clinics—that should take care of the elderly. The third step, we'll dismantle the schools—they must send the kids to school, you see. Alert social services. And then, if all of that doesn't get it across the line, we'll have to cut the water and power. Oh, but not for the courts or jailhouse. We'll have to keep those operational to manage unrest."

"Sir? Will that work? Are we... allowed to...?" Susan trailed off and looked down to her safety blanket of papers of the law.

"Look, we can't endlessly subsidise lifestyle choices if those lifestyle choices are not conducive to the kind of full participation in Australian society that everyone should have." Susan sank into her seat at the Chairman's response. "Roger, what is the position with the buyers?"

"As soon as our preliminary excavation confirms trace amounts, we will receive sixty percent of total payment from our investors abroad, with the remaining forty percent to trickle in over the next ten years as mining commences. However, we cannot excavate until the land has been vacated by its current inhabitants."

"Fantastic! That's fantastic news."

"Come on, let's go. We'd better discuss this," said Kojak, the pot plant in the corner.

The four transitioned back to the world above and found shelter in a cave among the timeless space, again observing the boardroom in their original form. The cave's walls were a thick red stone. A rough and jagged edge sprouted from its hard face.

"Who're they talking about?" asked Dom.

"Owl Totem," replied Koko.

"Oh no… then we should perhaps wake Walken."

The Wulgi froze time to discuss the matter at hand. The people in the boardroom below them remained still in their stuffy confines. Each of the Wulgi gently swayed as they hummed a soft tune in harmony.

They jolted from their trance, eyes wide open and glowing a deep golden aura. Kenny removed a large piece of quartz from his cloak and placed it on the table in front of the group. They surrounded it and watched its glow synchronise with the pulse of the drone.

"We have to wake Walken," they said collectively.

A clear white crystal began to morph on the walls of the cave. It sparkled all the way down the throat of the cave and started to beat with a soft glow. A drone rolled in on the breeze from a distance. Its pulse was faint, like the gust of a butterfly's soft wings, a delicate hope attached to each beat. The drone of the didgeridoo crescendos and consumes all other noises.

In the beginning, there was nothing. In sight anyway.

It was somewhere, all condensed into one. An answer that you know all too well, yet still seems to lurk just off the horizon of distant memory.

There were no pathways, no etched river tracks, no song lines. There was no song at all, in fact, only the voice. The land was completely smooth and flat—except for one mountain. This mountain, with its deep red skin, was as big as all mountains put together. The earth coiled on itself like a tightly wound cat, fast asleep in the warm sun.

The surface of the mountain cracked and groaned with steady rhythm. It rose as it expanded and cracks formed along the face. Then it would fall and they would be reunited. It inflated and deflated, the hard skin cracking and crumbling as the small stones danced. A deep drone sang from the mountain with its movement and it shook the earth.

She was sleeping that long sleep. The intensity of the drone shook the mountain and it began to crumble like a sandcastle. Cracks formed in the rockface and mountainous shards fell to the ground in an avalanche of suffocating red dust.

A red beam shot through the crack. Another hole formed on the top of the mound of earth as a giant chunk exploded into the sky and flew beyond sight. An orange light with yellow aura broke free from the monolithic site.

The base of the mountain, where the mounds

had fallen, began sprouting life all around. Lush grass sprang from the dusty earth and sprawled its growth everywhere. From the delicate blades twigs of brown shot up that quickly became trees with lush heads of thick green leaves. Bushes popped up like spots of accidental paint on the canvas of a clumsy artist.

A light blue hue broke free from the mountain. It shook like the cocoon of a butterfly emerging from its morphosis. It all crumbled. It fell thunderously, its debris flung as far as the horizon could project. Indigo and violet beams entwined and danced from under the rubble. From the centre of this pile shot a pure white sphere. All the light gravitated towards it and danced around it like a solar system, in perfect balance.

Together they went spinning around the loose rocks as they flung them everywhere across the flat unformed land. Where they landed, they made smaller mountains that towered to the sky. They were spinning so fast they cleared all the rubble from the mountain and spread it over the flat land. They rubbed against the side of the hill to scratch their backs.

A deep bass tone joined the rhythm of the drone.

Woophf... woophf... woophf

The sound was like a helicopter starting to spin its blades. The clouds began to convene in the sky above. This noise and pattern grew with intensity. Translucent faces appeared, suspended in the centre of their light.

Woophf, woophf, woophf, woophf, woophf, woophf

It completely consumed the landscape.

Woophf, woophf, woophf woophf, woophf, woophf, woophf, woophf, woophf, woophf, woophf, woophf

Walken was waking up.

A bright white beam projected out of the crumbling rock. Walken stood tall to the sky. All the wisps looked to her, continuing in their orbit and followed her lead into the atmosphere. She arched her back high into the sky and let her wisps play among the clouds. All that was left of the original landmass was the core, a single piece of red earth, smoothed and rounded from the whirlwind. This formed the red heart of the land.

Each wisp continued their orbit of Walken's

white light core. They danced and chased each other around and around like a helix, like a seed of creation.

Walken was thirsty from her long sleep and she went to find water. The fiery yellow sun licked at her from above with its scorching tongue. She sped west at an incredible pace, her wisps of light twirling and dancing as they flew. They jumped into the earth and wiggled through its crust. They etched valleys and riverways as they danced their dance. They played and weaved the landscape as they travelled in search for water. A tumultuous topography was left in their wake.

She dived into the ground and travelled beneath the earth's crust, lost in her dance. The land above rose to form a rocky mound that scraped at the ticklish sky. Trees leapt from the ground that Walken had raised, full of life. The white gums sprawled their fatal branches wide, their succulent green leaves and bunched honky-nuts perfumed the winds with an enticing eucalypt. The broccoli trees sprouted and stretched their branches far, with a long slender trunk standing underneath and an afro of puffed white flowered hair. Bushes overflowed from the soil and brought with them a healthy covering of grass.

Walken rose from underground and shot high

into the sky. At her apex, she surveyed all. The nothingness was consumed by the ripples that spread over the smooth and flat landscape.

Oh, isn't that pretty, she thought to herself.

She dived back towards the ground at full pace, her wisps of colour blurred with their haste. Walken, having so much fun, repeated her breakthroughs and dives, leaving polka dotted caverns in the earth. She started dancing. Walken danced her dance as the wisps looked on.

Woophf... woophf... woophf*

All the wisps talked and gawked as they learned Walken's creation dance.

"Whoaaa," said Mirda the wisp, "magnificent."

"Oooooooo," said Yoorda, another wisp, who slowly gravitated towards Walken like a moth to a light.

"What was that last move she did?" asked Yoont, fumbling to repeat it.

"Noo, it was like this," demonstrated Nodjam, who performed the move flawlessly.

"Move! Get outta my way!" bellowed Wooyan, eager to join Walken.

"I guess we'd better too," said the wisp Kawa to Viola.

They all orbited Walken and moved as a single helix. Their powers magnified in the united presence of one another, each supporting colour an essential player in the performance. They danced and they played under the clouds in the sky. These clouds, white and fluffy, drifted over to join the party. They came from all over and gathered high above.

"Oh, she's great! I've never seen dancing before!!!" gushed one of the clouds to his gaseous cohort, drifting in the flow.

"Look at her go! She's so free. Jiggered and jolting like that," admired another.

"Bravo! Bravo!" said a third.

The clouds filled with joy and began to cry with emotion. They poured rain to the ground where the droplets clapped against the dry dancefloor upon which Walken performed. The faint patter of the light drizzle accompanied her.

Woophf... woophf... woophf

Walken danced harder, and faster, having even more fun!

"Oh my! Bravo!!! Encore!"

The clouds let loose a downpouring ovation. Thunder and lightning erupted in the heavy applauding rain. A flood gushed over the land, filling the etched valleys, rivers and lakes of Walken's frolicking. The roots of the forests gorged their thirst on the liquid lifeforce. Within the same breath, seeds morphed to sturdy trunks with flexed branches, and grass grew taller and thicker, as if stretching from a deep sleep.

CRRACCK! screamed the lightning as it struck the tallest tree.

The thick jarrah trunk exploded and sprayed lethal projectiles all around. Fire clung to them; its heat burned through the rain. A warm aura glowed from the stump of the tree, no longer growing with the pace of the rest of the greenery.

"Hello, Crocodile," said Walken, her white core pulsating with every syllable. The wisps danced with excitement at the reunion.

Crocodile emerged nose first from the flooded tall grass. Puffs of air flicked the water from his rough skin.

"Walken! This is a lot of rain. You been dancin' 'gen?" grumbled Crocodile, in a crackly voice still being born into existence.

"There sure is a lot," said Walken. "Actually, more than I had planned. Heh. And over so much distance. I'll need to make sure that everything gets looked after, has enough to survive, but not enough so that others can't..."

Walken paused for a moment.

"Can you help me, Crocodile? Can I leave you in charge of all the waterways?"

"Of course. I can do that. But I can't do anything about those trees, or the flowers over there."

"That's ok. I'm sure we'll work something out," said Walken.

The bushes off to the side began to rustle violently.

"Ouch! Stop kicking me!!! I've told you so many times!" said a voice.

"I can't help it! You're too close to me. I'm a bouncer! I BOUNCE! It's what I do. You think I have a choice?" replied the first voice's adversary.

"Just roll left…"

The bush shook the Richter.

"The other left!!!"

"Just accept me for me!!!"

"Shh. Stop it!" whispered a mouse-like creature, "I think someone's watching us."

Walken parted the green veil of the bush to reveal the bickering marsupials. There was Kangaroo, Wallaby and Bandicoot, all contorted and tangled in the woven twig-branches.

"Oh, hey Walken. I didn't know you were awake. Can you get these two apart?" said the mouse-ish bandicoot.

Walken chuckled softly, "Come, you three. I need your help. I need you to look after the bushes, grass and plants."

"What about the mushrooms?" barked Kangaroo, untangling from Wallaby in the bush. "I love mushrooms!"

"Yes, and the mushrooms, but don't eat them all. Remember, the more you take, the less you'll have," replied Walken. "That goes for all of you!"

The rain subsided as the clouds became bored and dissipated their separate ways. A horde of small animals stampeded from the east. There were birds and bees, cicadas and beetles, snakes and lizards.

Goanna revealed itself from under the sand and wriggled over to the burning tree. The fire still crackled on the jarrah spears that had been carved from the lightning.

"Goanna, I know you've only just got here, but can I give you a job too?" asked Walken.

"You sure can!" he hissed.

"I need you to make sure these insects all behave. They'll be tending to the pollen and it's important they stay on track. Pesky insects, always getting distracted by their buzzing! They'll keep it trim and tidy and ensure everything is as it should be." Walken turned to the group, "Everyone, come around the fire."

The animals gathered and sat around Walken in a circle. Kangaroo, Crocodile, Cockatoo, Bandicoot, Snake, Goanna, Emu, the other birds and all the insects surrounded the blazing fire. In front of each of them lay a long jarrah fragment, a steady flame clutching at the end.

"You are the caretakers. I am trusting you all to ensure that this magical place flourishes with life and abundance. Take anything you need, except for more," instructed Walken. "Now, instead of just talking and talking, it's time for us all to give back."

The animals stood. As they rose, their fur and feathers morphed into squishy flesh. Their skeletons stretched and groaned into new shapes. Their organs shifted and slopped inside them, waltzing into their new positions. Long fleshy feet filled with a litter of bones popped out the end of the long slender legs. Thin bony fingers sprouted from the ends of their arms, quickly followed by a thick palm that blossomed out of the fleshy stub.

They clenched their fists and wriggled their toes and legs in the calibration of their new skin.

"Take from this original fire a torch that holds its light. As we take from it, we commit to preserve its creation and convene to maintain balance and harmony between the two worlds and all its creation—both living and non-living."

They each removed a flame from the original fire and ceremoniously retreated into the night without another word.

Only Walken and Crocodile remained in the central clearing. The fire had dulled itself down to simmer in the ashes.

"Do you think this time will be different?" asked Crocodile.

"Different?" she paused. "Oh yes. That. Well, it's going ok so far. Remember the times we didn't even get this far! I'm sure it will be different this time. There is only love and peace here now. And they understand their interdependence. I've given them everything they need in this magical land."

Crocodile slid casually into the shallow creek and blew bubbles out of his nose. They shattered the clear glass surface of the river.

"Hmmpf," Crocodile grumbled. "I hope you're right, old friend. Take care, Walken. I'll see you when I need to."

Crocodile vanished into the lake and began his eternal patrol of the spiritual waterways.

Walken had achieved a lot since waking up under the mountain. She went to find some shade under one of the newly grown trees. Their canopy joined the breeze in a relaxing medley. Her wisps passed freely through the trunks and roots of the forest and weaved in and out of the earth.

Walken circled an area below and coiled to rest on herself. She quickly faded into the limbo of suspended slumber.

Siggghhhhhhhh. What a relief.

PppffffffftttttttttPpppprrrrrrrrrtttt...squee-aak Walken accidentally let slip a thunderous fart.

What the hell was that?! Walken jolted from her limbo.

Squelch, squelch, squelch, squelch, squelch, squelch, squelch, squelch, squelch

Walken turned quickly to check behind her.

She spotted some muddy patches with heavily stamped footprints on the floor. They led east and were well over the horizon before Walken could get a clear sight.

The patches were printed with a firm heel that pressed all the way into the surface below. Four thick toe prints were stamped more softly into the mud.

Well... that wasn't meant to happen, Walken said to her wisps.

CHAPTER 2

The sun bled over the clouds that night, bringing with it news of the young boy's missing father. The cool air blanketed the gathering and soothed the heat of the day. The cicadas slowed in their rhythmic tick, commanding the evening to rise in preparation for the mourning of next light.

An eaglehawk flew high above the trees of the thickly bushed valley. Tall white gums reached their tattered branches to the cloudless blue sky. A canopy of plump green eucalyptus leaves stretched to the horizon. They clapped together and rustled in the cool breeze of the Djeran season.

Smoke rose from a clearing in the trees and the curious bird went to investigate. The eaglehawk tucked in its wings for descent and plummeted towards the ground. It spiralled through the sprawled branches, dodging each one masterfully. At the last moment before impact with the ground, it spread its wings with a tremendous huff. The dust and earth below fled with the strength of the breeze. And all was calm.

Eaglehawk hopped about on his grey, wrinkled talons. It scuffed the well-kept peace of the soil around the central area of the village. Burned logs rested in the white ash from the remains of last night's fire. A wide perimeter of stones circled the remains, with fine sand on the other side of its border.

"Ay! Shoo bird!" yelled a voice in its inherent local tongue.

The slick brown wings with white accents pushed the air beneath them and launched Eaglehawk away from the fire-pit.

"Gruuuuuuuel," muttered Eaglehawk deep from within her throat.

The humpies made of wood and foliage canopy gave good shade in the sun. Their raised platform, with sewn reeds for shelter, let the Djeran breeze play underneath. A soft air flowed through the beds and brushed against a small group of huddled men. They each had their shoulders hunched and muttered into the centre of their gathering.

"I heard they carried his body away. Found him out Badagurra way," recalled Jerra.

"Nah, I heard he's dead."

"What did you see? I've heard his skin was red

as. All over in spots like blisters. What did you see?" asked Freya, curious to compare hearsay.

"What I heard is that they poisoned him. On purpose, like," posited Terra.

"Ay? From who do you hear this?" asked Freya, continuing, "Who's they? What do they want with him anyways?"

"Who I heard it from, never matter. I heard his blood oozed black. Eyes all red when they found him. Thin pale skin. Blue lips." Terra shuddered at the imagery of his description. "Reckon someone killed him. Gave him the illness, let it eat away his spirit."

"Nasty stuff, that," added Jerra.

"I don't trust these clan meetings. There's one coming up you know. That explains all the unrest, I reckon. A lot of weird stuff happening with them sisters playing in the sky," speculated Freya.

"Someone will know. All the nations coming together. If they don't know about it, well, I don't know. You'd think all people together from every place could figure it out."

"Gotta make it right." Terra began to get more heated. "Gotta find out who done it and take one of them. Blood for blood, you know?! It's all gotta be equal before they come together."

Grandfather walked up to the small group, attracted by their secrecy. His wrinkled and hardened hands grasped their opposing forearm behind his back. A knot rested on the small of his back; as he walked, it bumped against him. A slight limp wobbled his step and he often enjoyed a yawn.

"What stupidity are you all kicking around in this circle, hmm?" asked Grandfather.

"You know, Grandfather. They killed him! We gotta kill too; otherwise, it won't be right," argued Terra.

"This was no murder, son. Calm your imagination from ill thought claims. The only thing we can be certain of is our uncertainty."

"How can we be sure? There has to be someone out there to blame!"

"Ahh, you seek blame too quickly, fool. And if you go looking for it, you will find it. Be it the truth or not. Now, keep your voices down. All your speculations of horror. The poor boy can probably hear you!" explained Grandfather.

Away from this group of four, over the carpet of gum-leaves and tender twigs, squatted a boy tracing a likeness with a short stick into the dirt at his feet. His chin rested heavily on his forearm, which was wrapped around his bent knee. The tip of the stick carved a trench in an oval and marked two ears on either side.

Ted, named after his father, lightly traced a triangle into the middle of the oval. He stared at the newly formed figure for a moment before extending his pinkie finger and gently erasing his first attempt. The grains of sand moved to his command until only the original oval, with its two ears, remained.

He poked two holes into the blank canvas of the earth. The figure now looked back into Ted. The two shared a space for a time. Tears began to well and blur the young boy's vision. They trickled over his eyelids with a compressed blink, as Ted traced an arched smile for his figure.

Ted's hand trembled with a mix of new emotions. In his imagination, he had crossed out the entire face with repeated vigour. He moved the stick back and forth through the dirt. The dust of his father's portrait coated his lungs.

He felt suffocated.

The face was not erased as Ted had thought. Instead, he found himself mindlessly spiralling curls atop the once bald figure.

Grandfather approached Ted, guided by concern. He looked over the boy's shoulder and recognised the rudimentary figure. A despairing breeze swayed the leaves and offered its condolences as it passed.

Mournful wailing bellowed over Karlaboodja, bouncing between the trees. A horrible moan of loss and screeching heartbreak. A helpless cry to nowhere.

"Come walk with me," directed Grandfather, "I have a restless story that needs a stretch."

Ted stood in stages. His hand boosted off his knee and hoisted his lazy body to its feet. Ted followed Grandfather with youthful obedience, yet his thoughts yelled over the conversation.

"Grandson, Makuru is coming. The cold winds and rain will be uncomfortable. The earth is going to a cold place, one of despair and suspense. But this is how it is able to grow, to flourish in the spring after the long nights. That is the way with change," explained Grandfather to an empty audience.

"Everything seems blue in Makuru," he continued, "there's a tinge over everything. It just can't be shook. Just have to keep moving with the flow of it all. The cold, the rain, the feelings of loss, all pass in time. But we have to go through them, my boy. We must go through them to grow. And appreciate the warmth when it returns."

"He's not coming back this time, is he?" quavered Ted in a hushed voice.

"That is not for us to decide, child."

"Where is he? People say he got sick. That he was in real pain."

"People say the first thing that comes to their head, boy. It is too early for that now, Edee. He rests well and surrounds you always." Grandfather offered his improvised advice to comfort Edee by any means. He stumbled through his words aimlessly in search of some joy in the boy's face.

"You don't know that, Grandfather," declared the smart boy. "Can I see him? If he's surrounding me?"

"No, child."

"Then why do you say these things. They're lies."

Edee continued to flick the dirt at his feet. He stabbed at it in frustration.

"What's Edee, Grandfather?" he wondered in a calm moment.

"You are, Edee," announced Grandfather, "we don't say your father's name anymore, Edee. But you'll always be my number-one, my yubba."

Edee walked for a moment in his new skin. Only yesterday he played in the innocence of childhood, unaware of the fear of uncertainty. A new light had brought with it a new life and jolted Edee into the rest of his existence.

The eaglehawk perched on a branch ahead of the pair. Thick brown feathers with a sturdy hooked beak. Its legs were defined, beyond stick-like talons with the strength to carry its weight thrice. It moved its head with immediacy, flicking from point to point. The bird looked at Edee. Edee looked at the bird. They shared a moment in the space between them.

A moment of complete recollection, a total connection, like passing a familiar face in a sea of people.

The bird shuffled along the branch with a noticeable limp. It shook the branch heavily in its hobble.

"Ahh! Look, grandson. Warlitj. He brings messages from loved ones," imparted Grandfather, comforting the child with myth.

"What does it say?" asked Edee.

"He is fine, your father. Resting safely as I said. Thank you, Warlitj. Your presence is a comfort, truly."

The wailing was faint as they walked further from camp.

The eaglehawk stretched its wings and pushed off its one good leg and fled deep into the night.

"Your mother sings her sad song, her wal sing," began Grandfather. "She sings to his memory and to his spirit. Mourning helps us all to move forward. To acknowledge loss. And change. Do you understand, child?"

Edee grunted, not wanting to talk anymore.

Grandfather turned and spotted Tilda, a young girl of Edee's age, following them at a modest pace. He put an arm around the boy's shoulder and pulled him in close.

"Your initiation will be brought forward," Grandfather responded quickly. "You're to become a man. And with it comes change again. New duty, new law… responsibility. It's a lot, I know. I'm sorry, child."

Grandfather stood, readjusted his coverings and walked back to the humpies. For he too had been young once and liked a girl.

Edee remained still for a moment to digest this whirlpool of circumstance. His mind, silent of emotion, now just repeated verse of songs in his head without thought. Incomplete fragments of music played in the silence. Edee felt nothing.

Everyone had kept telling him that he ought to be sad. Yet, in that moment, nothing was more comfortable. He thought he might be broken. He missed his father, of course, but found only vacancy where those outside expected sorrow.

Tilda walked up to Edee delicately. Her soft footsteps snuck her closer without detection. She sat on a fallen log by the trail and watched. The wailing had settled again and dominated the silence. It pierced Tilda with deep sympathy.

"Hey! Come sit," beckoned Tilda.

Edee was jolted from his trance with the crash of a wave of nerves. His throat tightened to make way for his heart and his palms cried a light sweat. He stumbled over to the log and sat on its far end. Tilda, unaccustomed to boyish stubbornness, went and sat closer to him.

"You ok?" consoled Tilda.

"Yeah," he replied in a grunt, with a sniff and wipe of his nose.

"Aunty says your born again is coming up. I dunno what she called it, something different. Are you scared?"

"Of what?"

"Walken. Big scary thing. Aunty say he's going to eat you up!"

"I wanna be eaten up. I don't wanna live here anymore." Edee welcomed the thought.

"Aunty also say you'll become a man. Like a whole new person, she reckons. Like you going to learn about all the adult things."

A moment passed them as they stared into nothing. A quietness sat beside them on the log.

"Sorry about your Dad," Tilda broke through the silence, her voice gentle.

She shuffled a little closer to the emotionally locked boy, her knee briefly bumping against his. Edee's mind raced with the contact. It was like soft lightning had struck his leg and rested in his thumping chest.

"I…," muttered the boy. I think of you, Tilda, always… He finished in his mind.

"What, Edee?"

"I thin…"

"Edee! Edee, WHERE ARE YOU?!" screamed Aunty with intent. "Edeeeee! Ah! There you are! We need more wood. Get on it now. Is that Tilda? Tell her to get the kids ready for evening's meal."

Yelling in her whining voice as always, Aunty barked her directions over everyone.

"And make sure you clean their hands!" she yelled as she turned back to camp. "Lazy kids. Sitting around yabbering while I hobble around. Typical. My Aunty would have never…"

And her noise settled in the distance.

"I better go. See ya, Edee."

"See ya, Tilda."

Edee sat alone again and watched as she walked away. He heaved his weight from the log and went in search of wood.

Make sure it's dry, now. The voice of Grandfather instructs him from his memory. You'll need thin sticks, even some dry leaves to get things started. You can strip bark if you need to for this. Look for the darkened grey pieces; they burn real good. If you knock on them, and they sound hollow, you've got it. Then find larger pieces—make them the brown wood with red tinge through it. That burns the best and longest.

Edee soon had both arms full of dry, thin twigs

and larger shards of jarrah. He trusted his feet to hold the imbalanced weight and correctly guide him home. The soft sand swallowed his steps. Edee stumbled, clunking the wood together. After finding his footing, much like a first-hour fawn, he continued to navigate through the surrounding bushland.

A whistle behind him made his head turn with instinctive security. Another whistle came from in front. Heavy footsteps from the right—no, the left—charged at him.

"Oh, hello Uncle. You scared m…"

"Edee, don't panic. Try and relax," interrupted Uncle.

Whoompf!

Edee's head was covered in a small woven bag. His arms and legs were bound, and he was carried over the threshold of youth and thrust into responsibility.

CHAPTER 3

A full moon had been and gone many times since Edee was taken from Karlaboodja. It was dark when they returned. Uncle led a group of four young men back from the sacred area used to initiate boys since the first stories were told. Edee's hair had grown long and thick, ahead of its natural course. Each new man wore a mane of woven reeds that topped their heads and brushed against the small of their back. On the front of these were palm-sized circular insignias designed and painted by the boys.

The markings reflected each of the men, inspired by their experiences of childhood. It symbolised what they were moving beyond and what would always remain with them. The drawn memories dangled over their foreheads and rested on the bridges of their noses.

Edee's long curls bounced against his shoulders. His belt carried a leather pouch, short spear, woomera and a shield the length of his forearm. All of these were crafted with careful diligence. He had invested the time into his tools and walked with this accomplishment.

Over Edee's left shoulder was a collection of two goannas and two bush fowls. He was the smallest of the group by quite a bit and was not able to carry much before getting tired. The largest boys carried their game, some with six or seven bush fowls and another with a wallaby.

Another boy carried a long spear that was as thick as a hundred-year-old tree from the young woods. A sharpened stone was mounted on its tip. He had come from another place to be initiated with the Karlaboodja boys. He was the largest person Edee had ever seen. The boy's veiny skin stretched over the size of his muscles that tensed to carry the weight of five goannas and seven bush fowls. He walked with a broader stride and stood two shoulders taller than Edee.

Over his right shoulder, he carried a fully-grown Kangaroo. Its weight would have slowed anyone else, but this boy bounced along on his toes as if unencumbered.

The group arrived at the central part of Karlaboodja. Everyone gathered around them to welcome their return.

"Masks off, boys," instructed Uncle, "and reveal to

us, men."

The men removed their headdresses and revealed their new selves to the crowd. The now men stood there awkwardly, swaying in all the attention. Soft smiles cracked the faces of those familiar in the gathered crowd.

Once dismissed, Edee broke away in a snap and walked from the gathering towards his mother's humpy. She had not been with the others to greet him. A voice cried from over his shoulder.

"Edee! Edee!! Wait there," shouted Grandfather from the crowd. He shuffled his aged frame towards the newly born Edee.

"Go ok?" Grandfather asked when he had caught up.

"Mmm, sure, it was fine," Edee lisped. He brushed his tongue over the vacant space of his gum where his front tooth was once stationed.

"Ahh, don't worry about it, chi——" Grandfather stopped himself. "Don't worry about it, Edee, you'll get used to it fast."

"My hands are raw," Edee said, rubbing his red and blistered palms together.

"Good skills to have. You'll get better at it. And your hands. They'll get stronger, unfortunately, the more you hurt them. Funny that," Grandfather chuckled.

They both stood still on the path and listened to the murmuring of the crowd in the background.

"I better get this to Mum," Edee interrupted the silence.

"Right. On you get."

Edee continued towards his mother's humpy. The last time he'd seen her was in the hysteria of his father's disappearance. He arrived at her humpy and slowly walked in.

"Kaya, Kaya, Edee." She moved to embrace him but held herself to her front foot.

"Kaya, mother," he replied.

Her eyes darted over his nose and eyes as she traced her affection through her baby.

"Oh, my boy. How are you?"

"I'm fine," he affirmed, rubbing the tender spot on his upper lip. "I've brought some food. I'll leave it here and be back later to prepare it."

"Haha, you're going to make a meal for me? Well, I'm not sure if I should be looking forward to it or dreading it."

"Then I guess you'll have to wait and see," said Edee through a front-toothless cheeky grin as he exited her room.

Tilda was waiting for him outside his mother's

humpy.

"Hey, Edee!" She sprang on him. "How was the bush? What'd ya see? Any spirits out there? Grandfather always telling me stories about them."

"Good," he replied with a boyish grunt, still fighting through a swollen bubble in his throat.

"Well? Tell me stuff! Share. Share!"

"I dunno. It was good to learn the stuff I did. Oh, look at this, it's so gross."

Edee lifted his lips and showed the vacant front tooth spot. The rest gleamed in their pearly white shine.

"Ahh, yuck!" Tilda retorted at the red and raw gum. "Now you look just the same as the older boys and they all stink."

Edee chuckled with Tilda.

"Here, bush fowl and goanna. Take them for you and your brothers," offered Edee.

"What about you two?"

"We've got the rest. I'm actually pretty good at catching goannas," Edee chuffed. "I can always get more."

"Aunty tells me I gotta go away," Tilda blurted through the small-talk, revealing the true intention of her ambush. "Tells me I gotta go live with the Bindjarra country, them Crocodile people."

"Wh… when?" shuddered a stunned Edee. He

had been enjoying the distraction of the meaningless small-talk.

"Don't know. But she tells me it's gotta happen soon. Something to do with the moons and flowers."

Edee let out a sigh through his nose. How different he had expected things to turn out. Childhood seemed a dream away.

"Tilda! Tildahhhh!!" yelled Aunty. "Tilda come here! Get away from Edee!"

"I gotta go, Edee," whispered Tilda as she hustled to get back to Aunty.

Bye, Edee thought as he let out a deflating sigh.

———————

A crowd gathered later in the evening, twice the size of the welcoming party. They huddled around the bora ring. The audience combined their soft conversation to create a faint rumbling of noise.

This attracted Edee, who had been walking around on the trails. He joined the back of the crowd without disturbing the combined conversation. He wiped his nose with his hand and rubbed his hands on his durdadyer pants.

A man stepped into the clearing and a tremendous thud rumbled the ground. The audience faded their babbled conversations, like a tuning orchestra before a performance.

The man's second step did not touch the ground. His dress was extravagant: a feathered headdress, coat and shorts to his knees, all made of feathers. White eyes were painted on his face. They were wide open and stretched wide from his forehead to his cheeks. He controlled the audience in this moment.

The story began on the teller's command. He took the audience to the thick reeds by a distant river of their imagination, where the fish flowed through the veins of the land. He introduced three men. Fisher-men. One of whom had a secret.

Three men stood with their knees just above the surface of the water. They could feel it cling to the dry hairs on their legs.

They had been waiting patiently, still, amongst the current of the water, watching the school of fish below.

One of the men spied his target and poised his short spear behind his ear, ready to fire.

The storyteller acted out these motions with delicate precision. The fine soil around him splashed as he flicked his feet in the imaginary water below him.

His eyes opened wide from under his painted mask. He extended his arms towards the audience with fingers spread apart.

Tension built in the audience as he parted his arms to reveal their full span to the audience.

The storyteller's arms, still with fingers widespread, dropped and he slapped his hands against his thighs. He let his fingers relax and sway in the water around his characters.

Only one of the fishermen was in the water as the day grew older. He traced his fingers over the surface of the water, feeling its elastic tension against their tips. The other two watched on from the shore as they gutted and cleaned their catches.

The lonely fisherman watched the fish and studied their movement. It was unclear which was leading the motion of the others. Or, in fact, how was it possible. Without communication, they flick left and glistened the sun against their scales. Then, with a flash, they shot to the right. They flailed their tails in sync and all matched the speed of each other. It was captivating. There was a meditative quality to fishing that rang true in this instance of contemplation.

The overlapped scales made a magnificent symphony of coloured refraction, which only shone in the fish that swam. Their brothers that lay on the banks of the shore no longer glistened as they had the morning before.

The other two laughed at the one in the water. They made fun of him behind the reeds and imitated his unortho-

dox techniques.

"You can't use your hands!" they laughed.

SPLASH

The two stopped laughing and went to see if he'd caught one with his strike.

The storyteller touched his fingers together at their tips and raised them to eye-level. He peeked over their created horizon. His eyes opened with amazement.

The two men on the shore looked over the curtain of reeds in search of their mysterious partner. The third man could not be seen.

"Bunyip!" screamed one of them. "Bunyip has taken him!"

The other huffed and panted in panic. A strong river current picked up the school of fish and carried them away.

"He's got his spirit! I told you we shouldn't have come here! We've gotta get back!"

They rushed to collect their things and quickly bundled them in a hurried bunch under each arm.

"Come on! Come on!" implored the first. "We gotta get help! You know what'll happen if Bunyip's got him, his spirit is captured and he can't come back to the physical *world!!! That Bunyip, he steals their power from their souls. They get weak, but he gets strong. The more souls he captures before they can be put to rest, he gets even more power."*

Their toes clutched at the rugged ground and launched them forward with high speed.

The storyteller brought these events to life through emphatic animation. Each stride was projected with a jolted hop to kick up the dust for added effect. He pushed away the imaginary branch in front of him, and his chest rose and fell with exaggeration. His characters were exhausted from the immediacy of the situation.

They stopped back at camp, hunched over and gasping for air. In an attempt to gather themselves, they began talking in between inhales.

*"We just saw—" *gasssp* "—Bunyip take him,"* started the first.

*"Took him right—"*gasssp*"—right down into the water,"* added the second.

*"We gotta—"*gasssp* "—go back and help. Get everyone—"but he never finished, interrupted by shock.*

There, across the newly lit fire, was the mysterious man. He was standing in front of a wooden rail with eight fish, all cleaned and gutted, ready for the meal. The white of his eyes glowed brightly from across the camp. The two men stood in stunned amazement and dropped their catch and equipment into the dirt.

"You…," uttered the first fisherman, pointing at the third.

———

The audience looked back stunned as theories played through their minds.

Out of the silence, the storyteller whispered,

"Ka-da-chi."

The shocked gasp of the audience inhaled the word.

The audience scattered in sections, like an icecap parting in the summer sun. The performance sat in their minds and played with their imaginations. People babbled about the storyteller as they drifted apart.

"A shape-shifter?" asked one woman to another.

"It couldn't be. Like, be in one spot one moment, then another the next. I've heard stories of that before," she replied. "Some say they travel with the wind, kicking up a willy-willy in their path. That could've been how he got back so quick?"

"But how did he get the fish?" interjected a third critic.

"Ahhhh," they all said in unison.

Edee drifted away from the group to join with

Grandfather who walked alone towards his humpy. His hobble rested in his right leg. Often the pain could be suppressed with a grunt, a rub and a gentle smile. But this time was different.

"Need a hand, Grandfather?" Edee offered in kindness and reached around Grandfather's shoulder.

"No no no! I can get there on my own," Grandfather snapped, sighed and groaned. "Everyone doing everything for me already. Can't even trust me to walk?"

"Sorry, Grandfather. I… I…"

"I know. Just—" *sigh* "Come on, now that you're here, I want to show you something. This way."

Edee was curious to know more about Kadachi and thought on the matter while they walked. Grandfather, too, walked silently; although his mind had long been vacant of curiosity.

They continued like this for some time until they reached their destination. Grandfather pushed away a large overhanging palm that looked to have fallen on the side of the track. It revealed a stout purposeful stone; white ochre traced three horizontal wavy lines that signified the area.

As they pushed through the bordering foliage, Edee thought of how often he had passed this spot as a boy. Oh, the fun he would have had in the towering branches and thick coverage, which would have been made grander through his youthful eyes.

The path trailed deeper into the bush and bent itself around a large boulder. Edee skimmed the soft skin of his palm against the coarse surface of the bleached grey rock. He gawked at the tremendous size of the thing and thought of all those before him who had stood exactly where he was, grappling with transition.

The area opened itself to Edee as he turned and passed the large boulder. Its ground was sunken deep; trees grew from its base that only scraped the breach. What Edee had thought were thick green bushes were, in fact, the treetops of thousand-year-old karri trees. The limestone walls that stretched high up and arched over dwarfed those that rested here.

A cool breeze spooling in the cavern blew past Edee. Its chills raised his skin and settled with his simmering anxiety. All around the grounds were small fire pits designed for recreational conversation and connection. Over to the side sat three middle-aged men, mumbling their deep rumbles to each other. Grandfather and Edee sat by their own fire, and Edee began to light it.

The whole place was amazing. Edee fumbled through stacking the tinder as he continued to look around in wonder. He crumbled his stack for the third time and sighed a loud sigh.

"You're distracted. Can't even get a fire going! Ha ha," teased Grandfather.

"It's not that. Well, it is, but…," stammered Edee. "What is Kadachi, Grandfather?"

"Huh, there's that eaglehawk again," he replied, distracted from the question. "What did you ask, Edee?"

"Kadachi, Grandfather. What do you hear of him?"

"Kadachi? He's the healer. He's the priest. He's the guidance from the spirit. People say he is magic," explained Grandfather. "But I'm too old to believe in such things."

"What stories have you heard of them?"

"Oh, plenty. Not all are true though. That's what makes it a bit tough. I hear they speak all languages in one voice. Universal tongue, they said. People think they can teleport from one place to another in just a flash. I've heard another say they can breathe under-water for as long as they want. He said he saw one go down for nearly a whole season and came up fine." Grandfather chuckled to himself. "Some people even think they can shapeshift—" he broke off to laugh "—into other animals!" He laughed again.

"But, what do you think, Grandfather?"

"Unfortunately, I think they're just stories, my yubba. But then again, what is real and what is story?"

"What about the villain?"

"Villain? I heard of no villain?"

"Sure, the bunyip."

"Oh, heh. Well, remember this, Edee. No one is the villain in their own story."

Grandfather slowly raised himself from the ground with creaks and groans.

"Our purpose is simple, Edee," stated Grandfather. "The universe has put us here as a manifestation of itself to care for the Earth. There's no other motivation than that. Maintain harmony and balance."

A group of young men, old enough to know it all, were laughing and running about the area. One of the flamboyant revellers, looking back at his friend, collided with Grandfather. The collision sent the old man firmly to the floor. Grandfather's fist-sized dilly bag, a weaving of hair and bark, dislodged from his belt. The contents of the pouch, quartz gems and coloured stones, trickled over the ground like droplets of a rainbow.

The boisterous laughter halted immediately. A shocked wave of silence crashed over all those around. The young men rushed to Grandfather's side. Edee collected the stones and gems, remembering his father's similar collection.

The light from a large quartz stone captured Edee's vision and dimmed reality. His eyes glazed over as he slipped into the stone in a mesmerised fascination. It had a natural hole bored smoothly in one side and out the other. A fixation grew within him on this magical stone. Its radiance filled him with fear, passion, desire and warmth. He took it in his hand and clutched at the heat coming from it. The warmth built in his palm.

"Ouch!" Edee squealed and quickly popped the stone in his dilly-bag. He quickly put the rest of the stones back in Grandfather's pouch.

"Sorry, Grandfather! Sorry, sorry, sorry!!!" apologised the distracted young man, fearing he had shattered the frame of the old man.

"You bloody idiot. What the heck are you doing?" Grandfather said with a head of steam. "Unbelievable…"

There was a time where Grandfather would have unleashed a fury onto the man, but on this occasion, he held his tongue.

"Come, Grandfather. I'll help you back home," said Edee.

"You better…" Grandfather looked sternly into the eyes of the offender. "Sleep well… I'll speak to you more in the morning."

The words sent shivers up the young man's spine.

"Yes, Grandfather," he said politely and went to join his group.

Grandfather leaned on Edee and they made their

way through the curtain palm onto the trail to Karla-boodja.

"You're an adult now," Grandfather said after the situation had faded from his mind, "time to start contributing more."

"Sure. You want me to hunt more?"

"Oh, no. I've seen you hunt. We have plenty of people to do that. No, we need a trader."

"A trader?"

"You see, the soil of Karlaboodja is not like the soil in other countries. Karlaboodja is littered with gems. And these other countries need these gems."

"Why do we give them gems?"

"We give them gems because we too need things in return. It's how we all help out. You understand?"

"How do I trade from Karlaboodja?" inquired Edee.

"That's just it, Edee. It's time for you to leave. To travel the lines of the trail songs and experience their winds and turns yourself."

They arrived at Grandfather's humpy.

"I'm fine from here," said Grandfather. "We'll talk more next time I see you."

Grandfather shuffled off into his bed and relaxed into a deep relieving sigh.

Edee walked through the central clearing on the way

to his bed. His eyes were red and dry with weariness. The day stretched beyond the sun's glow and rest seemed a welcome dream.

"Edee!" Tilda whispered in a restrained type of yell. "Edee, hey, psst."

"Tilda? What're you still doing up?!" Edee matched her urgent whispering.

"Come 'ere", she instructed.

She took his hand and the pair scurried away as sneaky children do after hours. Their hurried footsteps rustling the earth were amplified in the silence of the night.

"Edee… I…" Tilda regained her breath. Her heart raced and thumped hard in her chest. "Edee, I'm leaving."

The words struck Edee as a hammer does the back of a skull. They resonated deep within him and repeated a thousand times in those few moments.

"What do you mean? Since when? Where?"

"Aunty told me. Says it's the way things are. I'm going to Bindjarra. Crocodile country."

"Well… what do I do?!"

"I'm sorry, Edee. Aunty says it isn't final yet."

"But… I thought we'd be together forever. I pictured it already. Thought really hard on it." Edee rubbed his welling eyes.

"What do you mean?"

"Together. You know. Like, *together*"

A familiar silence sat beside them. Edee wasn't entirely sure, either, what he meant by 'together'. He had understood that mothers and fathers were together, and he wanted that. He wanted Tilda.

"I'm sorry Edee. It's not my choice. But I don't have a choice. You know?"

Edee knew, but let frustration and anger dominate.

"Yeah. I know," he said sombrely. "I better go."

He left in a huff, running from the situation.

"Ok, Edee," whispered Tilda. "Hey, Edee… I'm sorry. I wish it weren't so."

CHAPTER 4

Edee was down by the creek sifting through the thick reeds that bordered its shore. He crouched down and rested his elbows on his bent knees. A fastidiousness had overcome him and rested in his furrowed brow. The mania calmed Edee and distracted his growing mind from its recent traumas.

These needed to be made just right. His hand weaved through them and reached for their roots. Edee grasped a handful and yanked them from their sandy home.

He took them to the grassy bank and shook them of their soil. The roots flailed violently like rag dolls. He laid them out in front of him one at a time for inspection. They looked like green soldiers at atten-tion. Edee rubbed them between his fingertips.

Too thin, he thought. This one too.

There's one! He picked up the plump reed and placed it away from the others.

*This one too. And that one. And this one for the high-
light.* Edee plucked a reed that had been bleached
white in the sun. He had discussed it with himself
and had chosen the best reeds for his craft.

Edee left the rejected reeds sprawled on the ground
and he walked over to a fallen tree. The log had been
purposely set in its new position as a rest area. A
large chunk formed a lounging seat and created a
comfortable workspace for Edee to craft. He lowered
himself into the seat, his knees holding his weight at
chest level.

*Pinch your thumb and index finger on either side of
the spine,* his Grandmother's voice spoke from his
memory. The tone and rhythm of her voice had
sung to him from birth. Her voice crackled over her
throat, resonating a tinny ring in Edee's memory.

*Pull apart softly. You wanna get all that long piece. One
strand. It's all about strands. Then we have a lot of them.
All laid out.*

Edee had deconstructed the once thick reeds into
fibrous strands of material. They lay there, slimsy and
weak all alone.

*Now take a small group of them. Not all of them, just a
few. Weave them back into one another. See? Like this.* Edee
saw himself sitting with Grandmother as he had done
years before, the strands becoming entwined in one.

Keep them thin. So that you can fit more of these

grouped strands together. Makes it nice and strong. Then you do the same, but with the ones you just made, see. Like this.

Edee bundled the three woven strands he had combined from the smaller fronds and bound them together. His hand searched in his dilly bag for the gem he sought. The coarse surface of the others brushed against the ridges of his fingertips.

That's not it, he thought. *Not that one either.*

A smooth chill touched him, crashing over his skin like a freshwater wave. *There you are.* He revealed the green woven necklace, with a beautiful white strand dancing amongst them, to the world. The sun reached into the quartz and refracted out in all directions. Its warmth rested in Edee's palm affectionately.

The thread, now woven four times over, was unbreakable in its union. Edee slid one side into the naturally formed hole of the gem and bound the two ends together. He paused to marvel at his creation. The quartz pulsed a soft glow as if giving a small wink.

Thanks, Grandma, he thought.

———————————

Tilda was away from the centre of Karlaboodja at this time. Not too far to be lost, but far enough to remain unfound. Dirt clung to the all grasping carriage underneath her fingernails. She had been digging, you see. Not a deep hole, just deep enough. Tilda had ground the seeds the night before, which were now piled in a mound of flour.

Lemon myrtle, a bit of rose plum, oh! And those pepper-corns he likes, she thought as she compiled her ingredients.

The mixture became runny after Tilda added the water to it. It sloshed about the bark-made bowl as her hand tumbled the dry material about its bath. There it goes, she thought, and the worry of adding too much water left her. The mixture thickened to a dough and smelled of spicy wildflowers.

Four large leaves, thick in their green colour and wide sprawl, were laid out on the ground in front of her. Tilda poured the dough onto the bed they made. It thonked out as one lump and was caught perfectly by the leaves.

Tilda thought of her travels ahead. A nervousness struck her stomach. She felt it seep over her insides like a thick crude oil spill in the ocean.

Tilda continued through the discomfort and wrapped the leaves to close the parcel of seasoned dough, placing it in the hole she'd dug before. She sprinkled its light covering with the hot coals from the past evening's fire. They crackled in the fresh air of the morning when Tilda added more wood to their glow.

For now, she waited in the company of her own voices.

The sun beat its warmth from the tallest point of the sky. Brighter than it had been for some time as the sun bounced off all angles. Edee squinted his eyes at the refractions from the soil around his travel pack. The open leather carrier held a swag of items: small tools, food and survival equipment.

Edee fastened his woomera to his belt. He closed his swag pack and threw it over his shoulder to test its weight. A few quick bounces on the spot and Edee took the load off to place it on the floor.

As he bent down the breeze kissed him with the smell of Tilda. Edee looked up from his pack to see her standing just beyond the humpy nearby. He bent down once more to rummage about in his things, taking the necklace in a tight ball concealed in his closed fist.

"Edee," Tilda said softly, "when do you think you'll be back?"

"Not long. Says Grandfather anyways. Just gotta go on the first round, to start," Edee replied.

"How far is it to the next peoples?"

"However long the songs are. It just takes as long as it takes. What's that you've got in your hand?"

Tilda slowly presented the leaf wrapped damper in

her ashy hands.

"I made this for your trip. You can't eat it all at once. Be rolling about those song trails. Be sure that you have some water. I had some earlier, not from this loaf, but from Aunty's and it got stuck in my throat. Felt like I couldn't get it down at all! Started panicking. Then I had some water. Slid straight down. Could feel it too!" Tilda exploded with conversation.

"Thh… thanks, Tilda." Edee reached out to take the damper from her hands and watched the necklace slip from his grasp.

Edee jolted for the necklace and dropped the damper. It hit the floor and rolled out of its leafy covering over the dirt at their feet. The necklace had hit the ground with a shattering thud and had submerged in the loose soil below. It had flagged itself with its exposed woven string.

The moment stood in time, as embarrassment tends to do. Meanwhile, his mind made a vivid recording for cringing recollection.

Edee scrambled for the damper. He picked it up and frantically shooed the dust that had hung on, blowing at it ferociously. Saliva misted the loaf in his emphatics. Tilda chuckled delicately at his show.

Tilda gently touched her fingertips to her lips and playfully laughed at his misfortune.

She looked down to see the necklace submerged

in the earth. It resonated a soft frequency through the ground, its steady thump tickled her feet. Tilda could see the gentle light that Edee had failed to notice. She slowly gravitated towards the stone in a trance. Edee's panicked search was muffled by white noise in her mind.

Tilda reached out her hand to pick up the necklace and the earth that covered it parted for her embrace. The stone glowed more vibrantly when it nestled in her palm. It should have felt white hot, yet Tilda caressed its energy effortlessly. Her heart thumped heavily in her chest. It called to her.

"What is this, Edee?" Tilda asked in a breathy tone of amazement.

He replied in a grunt, still mending the damper.

"Yeah, well, ahhh, it's for you. It's a stone I found. And I thought it was pretty. Had a natural hole in it. I made it so you can carry it. For your time with the Bindjarra... It's nothing. It's not as good as this damper though! That's gonna be delicious."

"Oh, it's beautiful. Thank you."

She put it around her neck and its heavyweight dissolved into the air, warming her chest against its touch.

"That's what I thought too. So, I thought of you."

Edee stood with a loaf of damper wrapped in frayed leaves. Tilda looked back with her gift clutched tightly and close to her chest. They peered through the irises of the other and viewed their beings.

They shared a moment with beating chests living in their future memories. Each watched it play out from outside themselves. Their affection lived a thousand lives in that span. From birth to death, through love and pain, they had shared an existence to last for eternity.

Edee mustered the strength for the first step. He fought against her magnetic attraction and summoned everything within him to go against his desire to surrender to its forces. The lump in his throat bobbled its uncomfortable self upward and pulled his mouth into a soft frown.

Once past the large overhanging tree, seven steps down the track, he exploded into tears. The lump had ruptured and sent a flood of sorrow pouring from his heart to his eyes.

Edee found relief after some deep breaths, making the pill easier to swallow. Ten more steps and he visited his most recent memory while taking a pinch of damper. He chewed it with an open mouth through a cheeky grin as he sniffed and wiped his runny nose. Edee had stepped out of the realm of uncertainty and he had nothing left to fear.

CHAPTER 5

In the world above, below, and with us now, the Wulgi stood confused.

"Wait, I don't remember it happening like that," queried Kojak.

"That... that was not pretty. Fleshy and bloated with thin dark hair all over," shuddered Kenny.

"Like a pig? I think I'm gonna be sick," gagged Dom.

"I don't think it's a pig. It looked like a hiccup. It can't be that bad," speculated Koko.

"One smelly hiccup," muttered Dom, under his breath.

"It missed the instructions!" exclaimed Kojak.

"It'll be fine. The others will take it in and provide for it and teach it how to survive in Walken's magic land," said Kenny.

"You're right. Love will sort it all out," comforted Kojak.

A large chunk of the original mountain flew through the air, propelled by Walken's dance. Its maroon skin blurred against the deep blue of the cloud-spattered sky. The boulder travelled all the way to the western edge of the land. The vacant plain whooshed below as if the globe itself spun beneath the suspended rock shard.

It hit the ground with tremendous force at gravity's request. A long skid was carved into the earth that trailed to its final resting place. A carpet of thick grass sprouted immediately in the skid. Trees and bushes quickly joined in the continuous growth. Life and forest stretched out from the land.

The trunks grew close to one another. They huddled to share their whispers. Thick grass trees filled the gaps between. The floor of the quickly growing forest filled with foliage and the deep red boulder of the first mountain became consumed by life.

Edee had now been travelling for three nights and had slept only once. The noises were very different out beyond his country. They bounced on the clear night air and danced in his imagination.

That sounds like a little girl screaming! he thought, jolted by the screech of a calling bird. It was day and the rays penetrated the green canopy above.

White clouds roamed the sky against its deep blue backdrop.

"COO-EE!!!" the sound, amplified between Edee's cupped hands, echoed over the trees. He trembled with the possibility of hearing a reply. Edee announced himself, as a non-threatening travel-ler, and secretly hoped for no reply. In this instance, there was no response. Edee moved on, relieved.

Edee found direction in the words sung before. His father's low rumbling voice hummed their tune in his memory.

Edee stopped to clear his throat once again.

"COO-EE!!!" the noise flung louder and wider than before. Edee sat and waited. For nothing. And he continued.

The tree trunks swirled a palette of white and grey. A dry air swayed the leaves above that trickled shade over the trail of compressed undergrowth. Over the bushes and between the trees a magnificent deep red boulder stood out. It was so large and its placement so peculiar, so alien, it was attractive in its obscu-rity. At its base was a vivid bed of blossomed flowers surrounded by tall growing grass. The trees closest were thicker, taller and stronger than those further back. A breeze of crisp delight welcomed Edee into its embrace.

He crouched with his tools to light the gum leaves. Friction was the key.

These fire spirits are ticklish, Grandfather would explain to the children. *So, what we do is we tickle 'em! Get them to laugh.*

"HAHA! COME ON, YOU CHEEKY SPIRITS!"

Edee placed a shaped wooden prod in a divot and held it with his left hand. He set the firestone in the middle, with its bored hole to guide the friction. He picked a handful of dried grass from the base of a nearby eucalypt tree and put it into the bowl of the curved shield. A calmness came over him. The calmness of ceremony.

With his right hand, Edee wrapped a woven rope of natural material around the vertical prod once and fastened the two ends to a bowed handle. As he moved his right hand back and forth, the friction of the prod began to smoke. His heart rate increased. He'd never gotten it to light first time before!

His hand frantically spun the ignition. Just when you think they are only sniggering, reminded Grandfather in the memory of his instruction, they laugh out loud as the Kookaburra beckons the sun. And the leaves caught fire; thick white smoke billowed from the shield.

Edee bathed the smoke over him. Memories of his upbringing accompanied him in the fire. Those who had educated him as he'd grown, the ancestors who had taught those before and all those back to the original words of tradition. The smoke cleansed the spirits of the area and ensured they would remain in their totemic place so as not to wander.

Edee felt them watching as he bathed in the smoky plumes from the shield. He emptied the material on the ground and stamped on it to extinguish it.

A heavy step now led Edee as he became wearier into the day. He left his arms to dangle at his side and did not seem bothered by the way they flopped around his body. His head bopped in a slump to the beat of his stride.

"COO-EE!!!" he grunted from a tipped back head.

The loose ground flew to dust as it was flung by Edee's dragging feet.

"COO-EE!!!" came hurtling over the unseen distance.

Edee froze.

His heart pounded. *Oh man. This is happening. Breathe. Breathe.* He cupped his hands to his mouth.

"COO-EE!!!" he replied to their reply.

What if they hate me? Are hostile or something. A different clan all together! Oh man . . .

Six travellers were resting on the side of the path by a body of water. They laughed so loud it was infectious. The joy beckoned through the trees. Edee grinned with relief and giggled at his carried away imagination.

Two men approached him, each with one palm raised facing Edee. He returned the gesture.

Their skin was etched with mountainous ranges of unique markings. Their chests were scraped with raised scars. The markings were all over their faces, down their arms and over their torsos. Edee had never seen people like this and he was captivated by their difference.

"Gaba Yaadha, traveller," said one of the men in a distant dialect.

"Um. Kaya?" Edee replied.

"Nooo. You idiot," said the other to his friend. "He's Karlaboodja. Look at those teeth! Your tongue still hung up on that place up north isn't it?"

"Ohh, yeah. Maybe a little," he replied. "Hey, friend! I'm Kolunga, this is Kalanga. Where are you from?"

Kalanga scoffed. "I just said! He's from Kar-la-bood-ja. Aren't you?"

"Yeah. Karlaboodja," confirmed Edee.

"What do they call you now?" asked Kalanga.

"Edee."

"Edee… Edee. Strange," said Kolunga.

"You thirsty, Edee? Want a drink?" asked Kalanga.

"Sure," he replied, numb to his thirst due to the excitement of the encounter.

The three walked some before joining with the others. Edee sat beside a young boy with the group. Edee leaned forward to say hello.

"He's ugly," blurted the boy, pointing to his own front teeth. "Got no teeth. Ha,ha,ha."

The young one was not marked like the two men that had escorted Edee.

"Where are you going?" asked Kalanga with no real interest.

"Trading. Grandfather tells me I'm off to Bilyakep first."

"I enjoy going to Bilyakep!" related Jilungo, one of the women sitting nearby. "It's so cosy there. Comfortable, I mean."

"They don't like me too much," blurted Kolunga.

"That's because you spilled a whole community meal last time we travelled through there, you bloody idiot!" exclaimed Kalanga.

"I didn't see it there! It wasn't my fault! Gah!"

Edee chuckled with a stern exhale out of his nose.

"What do your people hunt, Edee?" asked Kalanga.

"Emu mainly," Edee replied, while taking a sip of water. "Although I don't. I'm good at goanna. Ohh and bush-fowl. Sometimes I get birds too, but I'm still learning the bigger game."

Kalanga turned to a woman sitting beside him with the group and spoke in a language entirely unfamiliar to Edee.

"Mirra, go and get the cycad nuts out of the pack."

Edee watched the words tumble out of Kalanga's mouth. They made a fantastic sound and rang over Edee's ears like a beautiful song he could not understand.

Mirra returned after rummaging in their pack.

"Hold out your hand," Mirra ordered and Edee complied. "These will make your emu, not so fast, drowsy."

Her skin touched his and closed the small collection of seeds in his palm. Edee thought of Tilda. Mirra put the palms of her hands together and touched them against the side of her face like a pillow.

"You put these in the water where the emu drinks," explained Kolunga, "and they'll get all sleepy. Make them easier to catch and kill."

Kolunga may have lacked a certain capability with conversation, but none could question his mastery of hunting practices.

"You'll even be able to walk right up to them. Put the spear in deep. Not even need to throw," he continued.

Edee bowed his head graciously and felt it necessary to reciprocate their hospitality with a gift of his own. From his dilly-bag, he pulled a handful of red, black and yellow gemstones.

"Here, these are for you," he said, holding out his hand.

Kalanga inspected them for a moment.

"What type of seeds are these?" he asked.

"They're not seeds. They're stones. Gemstones."

"Oh. Well. Ok, thank you, I guess," said Kalanga politely, still unsure of what he held in his hand.

There was a confused silence. Edee was unsure what course of action to take next. He'd been kind, polite. That must be it.

"Well, I best make tracks," mumbled Edee, standing to leave in a hurry.

"Nooo, no. Edee. Tonight, we'll stay together and share this place on our journeys. Tomorrow we'll part, but for now, let's visit and let our stories bring in the morning," implored Kalanga.

Flatterd by the invitiation, Edee sat back down to a new comfort. The feeling of belonging calmed him and was welcomed in his difference.

CHAPTER 6

On her tour of the land, Walken met with Moorn Gooljak, the black swan in the west.

"Kaya, Kaya! Moorn Gooljak," she laughed with fresh joy.

"Kaya, Walken. Look at my flock! They are growing well. Thank you for the rivers and the water. And these wings!!!" enthused Gooljak. "Look how terrifying I can be."

Gooljak arched its long neck and positioned its head and beak like the handle of a large water jug. She sprawled her wings and hurried towards Walken, screeching.

"Pretty scary, right? I can't really do anything. Only nip. But I am pretty proud with myself," finished Moorn Gooljak.

"Ye—yes, very frightening." Walken politely agreed.

Walken sank herself into the earth as she moved north parallel to the coast. A huge chunk of land rose up from the surface and shaded all the area below. The wisps played in the surrounds and danced their dance over the soil. Green sprang from the sand and life was on its way.

She moved the earth playfully from beneath its surface. Walken wove herself in and out of it, creating a massive network of underground tunnels. She shot up from beneath the ground at the base of the mound she'd pushed up before and scraped along its vertical face. The wisps dipped themselves into the cliff and formed caves and crevices of the area.

Walken viewed her tracks from above. A small, determined stream of water pioneered its way towards the newly formed passageways. Up close, the surface tension of the water made it look as though a wall of water approached. It weaved its way into the small cracks that led to the larger gaps and poured into the lake beds formed by Walken's frolic. The stream grew in ferocity and water came from all around to join it as it leapt from the top of the cliff, down the vertical scrapings of Walken and down into the waterways below.

Bandicoot watched on from a distance.

"Wow, Walken! This is a beautiful waterfall! And I love these hills!"

"Oh?" Walken replied, "well, would you like to look after them for me?"

"Oh boy! I'd love to!" Bandicoot hopped over towards Walken.

The water had filled all the carvings and now rested calmly in the lakes. A waterfall babbled with a white haze and all was well. Walken and her wisps swam in the waterways and their colours seeped into the river at the bottom of the fall. This life force leaked through the water as far as the water flowed. All the waterways were clean and pure and fuelled the land with magic.

It was evening. Edee decided to continue a little further before resting. The distance between the trees had increased. Thick spinifex bushes dominated the gaps between the trunks, their long thin blades sprawled madly. Their ruggedness was lessened against the vibrant reds of the kurulbrang . The soil was now dry white soft sand that swallowed Edee's feet with each step.

A tree ahead had a sheet of bark carved out of it. Its thousand-year-old scar with welted border stood out clearly to the eye. It bore a sheet-sized recess, likely the scar of a thousand-year-old shield. Imprinted into the grown over trunk was a symbol warning of the upcoming community. It cautioned that there was a community ahead by the river. Edee had arrived at the outskirts of Bilyakep.

Edee made camp off the trail near the sign.

There are rules, you know, repeated Grandfather as Edee gathered his tinder and ignition. *You can't just go running up on someone's camp. No matter how wide your smile. They'll say, 'Look at this smiling idiot - kill him.' Maybe not. But don't just walk into another group. Let them know you're here. Let them come to you.*

Edee placed a shaped wooden prod in a divot and held it with his left hand. He set the firestone in the middle and placed a handful of dried grass into the bowl of the curved shield. A calmness came over him. The calmness of ceremony. He moved his right hand back and forth; the friction of the prod began to smoke.

An eaglehawk screeched from the cover of the night. Edee looked up to see its golden eyes pierce through the darkness and lock with his own gaze.

The fire crackled into the evening and shone its beacon clearly to those around. It was early in the night, but Edee, overcome with exhaustion and the comfort of a fire, immediately fell asleep.

He awoke the next morning before the sun. A loud river babbled its tune as the water rushed. Everything was a silhouette against the soft light of the sky. Edee lay on his back, covered in his deconstructed bag for warmth and gazed sleeplessly at the night.

The trees above and all below were jet black. Their cover bordered the stage for dawn.

The morning eased in gently. A soft blue played over a dark slate and the birds yawned to a new day. A whisper of blue flushed over the sky that veiled the stars. It was a magical time during which the light hums against the crisp air and harmonises with the fragrant eucalyptus.

What followed the blue was a joyful clashing of oranges and reds that sprawled across the horizon. The trees were fading from the night. All the stars were coloured over as the earth turned to the sun.

The birds began their chorus of the day. Their songs lifted the final shadows of the night and welcomed the warm glow of the new light over the horizon. They sang their tweets and chirped their beats, but there was one shadow that would not leave.

Edee stretched his arms wide and opened his chest to the morning breeze. His feet curled to the soil and he wiggled his toes awake. He scratched himself, let out a thunderous rumble and went beside a tree to pee.

After his morning routine, he gathered his things into his swag. Edee waited and stared into the distance.

"Oy, oy," shouted a voice from the south. "Where're you from?"

UNDER THE SHADE

A man wrapped in strands of blue material approached Edee with a long spear in hand. He resembled the large boy with whom Edee had been initiated. The man's shoulders were as big as Edee's head. Feathers clung at its tip in a bundle, each one a different colour. His eyes were fierce, hollow, large and white. They stared back into Edee.

"Karlaboodja. Trading, just passing through," replied Edee after clearing his throat.

"Right. This way. No warnings. Never seen your face before. Anything funny and you're done." The man quickly turned and walked back towards Bilyakep.

Edee collected his things and hurried to catch up with his escort. "Wait up!"

He's in a bad mood, Edee thought as he clumsily juggled his things that cascaded from his fumbled embrace. The pair walked off the path in the direction from which the escort had come.

"Which way are we going?" asked Edee.

"This way. Keep up," replied the man.

"What's your name?"

"Why does that matter? This way now. Watch you don't trip on that root."

"What?" asked Edee, as he tripped on the large exposed root and slopped face-first to the ground. Luckily, a bundle of hard objects broke his fall. The escort turned back, chuckled and continued.

"This way," he snapped, without missing a beat.

They broke through the border of the dense bush cover to find themselves atop a small incline. At the bottom of the valley ran the river that had woken Edee to the day. It was the largest body of water he'd seen and he marvelled at its power.

Beside the river was the community. Edee could see children playing on the outskirts and a gathering of adults by the central clearing. He followed the escort down into Bilyakep.

A central clearing served as the nucleus for the community. Strands of woven rope hung from their stands by the weaving stations. The platting was so elegant and intricate. Edee felt embarrassed comparing the necklace he'd woven for Tilda to these pieces.

The humpies here were a dome structure formed with a bound frame of flexible lumber, topped with a cover of entwined spinifex for shelter.

Lost in his curiosity about the dome humpies, Edee crashed into a girl carrying a collection of woven baskets.

"Oof!" she exclaimed, dropping her inventory and self to the floor.

A hot flush crashed over Edee. Oh, boy... he thought.

"I'm sorry. Sorry. So sorry. Sorry." He stretched out his arm in offer to help her up before collecting her baskets for her.

She smacked his hand away and shook her finger violently at him with tight lips. Apparently, she was giving him a piece of her mind, although no words left her mouth.

"What're you saying?" he asked, looking to his escort who, he realised, had abandoned him at the first available chance.

"Keep quiet!" she demanded, avoiding eye-contact, "you oblivious imbecile."

Edee looked out beyond the humpies at the people of Bilyakep. They walked sullenly and with great weight. Each person shuffled about their duties without sound. There was a gloomy vibe that rested in your chest like a kaleidoscope of nauseous butterflies.

"What's your name?" asked Edee, again offering his hand.

"My name? Fylia. Why does that matter? Eeurgh, actually. Leave me alone. I can't be talking right now." Fylia shot up to her feet, gathered her baskets and left in a hurry.

Edee stood alone in a country that was not his own. He looked to his left and then his right. With no clear way to go, he went straight in search of someone he could talk to who would not run away.

He had not taken two steps before a commotion erupted to his right. There were two women and a man standing around an animated little girl. Edee heard her story through her movements and, be it a conscious or unconscious decision, found himself drawn to the conflict.

"Enough!" shouted Angyla, the little girl's mother. "You foolish girl."

"I saw this!" proclaimed the girl "I saw this through mine eyes!! They took him while he made fire. I saw one, and one and one come after him and hit him with small logs." She counted out the ones on her hand to make three.

"Any more jibber jabber and you'll get a smack, girl. Ya hear?" said Ellyia, also the little girl's mother and disciplinarian.

"I'm sorry, Aunty. But I'm gonna take the smack. I seen this, they were Diemens, Aunty. Grandfather tells me about them in the stories. Big hairy face over their mouth. They had the blue hats too! Dirty and worn. Nasty yellow teeth. Crooked and sick." The little girl puffed her face and extended her arms out by her sides.

"One sit up on the hill, him have gold dots up his tummy. Fat one like this. They snarl at each other. Gurgled out their mouths. Oh, blue covers too. With silver dots all down their belly. Pointy white ears through a brown rag fur. SNARL! SNARL!!" She morphed herself into the beasts and impersonated their cloying sounds. "They Diemens like Grandfather says. I know it. They eats him whole. Spirit too. They just took him right away!"

"Pfft-eh. Ha-ha. Just stories, little one," laughed Agylio, her uncle. "Most of them are just made up. You can't take it all on."

"IT'S TRUE!!!" she replied in frustration.

Ellyia raised her hand and smacked Angyla hard across the face.

"Take some responsibility for this!" Ellyia said to Angyla.

"She doesn't even have her second teeth yet," Angyla replied. "She can't be responsible for these things. I know she can't be. She can't be spouting this nonsense around the family. Lotta tension already with the not knowing. Keep her in line, or you'll cop it."

"Everything alright with you, there?" Agylio asked Edee, breaking his illusion of audience.

"Me?"

"Yeah. You. Everything ok? You're just standing there."

"On my way through from Karlaboodja."

"Well, I'll take you to the person for that. Who're you? I'm Agylio."

"Edee."

"Edee of Karlaboodja. That sounds familiar. You're after the spinifex, yeah?" asked Agylio. "What everyone else comes through here for. Tindlio will help you. Done it a couple times before. Tindlio, this is Karlaboodja."

"Pretty good timing!" said Tindlio, gesturing his sweeping arm to the ground. "Please, sit."

Edee crossed his legs and lowered himself to the ground. The weight of his pack fell from his shoulders and his chest opened to a large breath of relief.

"We are pleased with the meat and tools you bring, but most of all grateful for the gems and relics you provide in this trying time for our country. She is sick. Those you passed to get to me feel it, but they do not understand."

"What's happened?" asked Edee, straight to the point and curious beyond polite.

"See, the thing with death is, we have a process for it. We have ritual and procedure. There is closure and we can all move on. The thing with disappearance is that no one knows what is going on! A man left Bilyakep on the trail and hasn't returned. Scouts went out to check if he's still in the country. Found his camp, but no man. Creepy."

Tindlio's eyebrows stretched high on his forehead wrinkling his perplexed skin.

"I wanna know what took 'im," he continued,

"people don't just disappear…" Tindlio tapped his foot at a twitching pace and sloppily chewed on the ends of his nails.

"They don't just disappear. That's evil spirit stuff. But what do we really know?"

Edee was stunned at this nervous outpour.

"Did you know his name?" asked Edee, fearing the answer.

"You know, I never did catch his name. Why's that, you know him or something?"

They both sat in the sombre silence that answers to the questions of existence. Tindlio stared, eyes wide, at the ground in front of Edee where clear droplets of quartz lay scattered. Warmth filled him as the gem refracted the light that shone in from the front opening.

"I'll need extra of these for the hunt," Tindlio insisted, snapping back to the purpose that brought them together. "Uncertainty is ahead of us and I fear these will be greatly needed to guide us through the dark."

Tindlio clutched a handful of the quartz and held them close to his chest. He took a deep breath, held it for a moment, and released it slowly back into the world.

"He was travelling those song lines too—" Tindlio hesitated, pausing in his sentence, unsure if his name can be spoken. "I'd be careful out there. There's something out there corrupting the path. Just… be vigilant, Edee."

CHAPTER 7

Walken was moving across the eastern coast of the land. The wisps played as they travelled like restless children. Again, they weaved into and formed the earth, orbiting around their central white core. Freshwater filled them from the artesian oceans below as if the hollow carvings of the riverways, streams and creeks were gashes to the skin. The spring of greenery quickly followed. White puffs of wavy-leaf hakea blossomed from the thin branches of the trees. On the ground, vibrant yellow sprang from the flowering acacia bushes.

Debris from the destruction of the original mountain had spread everywhere across the flat land and patches of lush forests now littered the rugged expanse. A thick treeline appeared on the horizon, but it was not complete. A brown decay had cut its growth. The canopy sloped away until there were only ragged stumps. Walken rushed to investigate the newly formed clearing.

The Wulgi watched from their platform in time.

"I wonder where the trees ent," sang Dom.

"It's 'went'. Push your lips together like this," demonstrated Kojak as he pursed his lips into a duckbill.

"Blah," Dom blurted, sticking out his tongue and miming eating it. "This tongue is in the way. Where'd they go?"

"You've heard this story before!" reminded Kenny.

"Not like this I haven't! None of us has. I don't even think Walken has," cautioned the now serious Dom.

There was silence among the group.

"Well… yeah, so. Let's go find out," Koko clearing his throat.

Walken circled above the brown devastation splotched in the canopy of green. It was a wide clearing and a perfect circle all around. The trees were gnawed down to their stumps and their remains reeked with halitosis. Branches that squashed the bushes and smothered the grass were recklessly thrown about. Trunks lay defeated on the ground, uprooted and exposed from their buried covering.

The soil had congealed and mixed with the chaff

of the vigorous shredding. The earth was leached and barren. A thin dust suffocated the land and a soft smoke clouded the air. It looked hard and unpleasant to Walken, who flew in for a closer look.

In the clearing, propped up against one of the fallen trees, was the hungry culprit. It snorted and grumbled a belch through its puffy pink lips, blistered by the harsh sun. Its fattened cheeks hung past its jaw and down to its second, even third, chin. A slight quiff of hair is pushed to the side and held with sweated beads.

The beast had fashioned a drab suit out of poorly sewn rags. A red vest struggled to conceal the giant bulging belly and a golden button strained under pressure. The thick pores that trenched his nose were clogged with soot. There were muddy footprints all around the clearing. A fat sole with three chunky toes stamped in the mud.

Walken approached cautiously.

"He—hey, what are you doing?" she asked delicately.

The beast gathered its breath with a huff and grumble.

"Clearing," he roared.

"But the trees aren't meant to be cleared."

"Well. They're in the way. Whatchya expect me to do? I need this space to live, you know."

"What do they call you?"

"They call me… ummm. Reginald D. Bunyip. Ahh, the third. Yes, that'll work. Just call me Bunyip," scoffed the beast through a crackle of saliva.

"It's the fart!" screamed Dom.

"The what?" said Kenny.

"That backend hiccup that Walken let slip," recounted Dom.

"He said he's Bunyip," stated Kojak.

"Oh, right. You believe everything you hear? Remember, I'm the clever man," continued Dom, impressed with his self-imposed title.

"You don't know it's the same. Let's give him the benefit of the doubt," suggested Koko.

"Pfft. Yeah ok… I know a fart when I see one and let me tell you, he's the fart," repeated Dom.

"What about the birds? And the other animals that were caring for the area?" Walken asked Bunyip.

"I dunno," he snorted again through his compressed snout. "Plenty of other bush. It's all the same anyway."

"It's completely different! Can't you see the Karri and Marri, and Jarrah and Tuart?!"

"They all taste pretty much like timber to me."

She began to feel sick with anger. It infected her stomach and spread through her blood.

"Forget it." She stamped in a quick beat. "Just don't clear anymore. There is plenty of room here now for you and no need to take from your neighbours. I'll have to keep my eye on you. The more you take, Bunyip, the less you'll have."

"Heh, that's a cute little saying." Bunyip shifted his weight forward and propped his legs on the ground under his hips. His thighs pushed heavily on his chest as he thrust himself to a stand and let out an awful wheeze.

"Eerrrugh!" *puff, puff* "An eye on me? Now there's no need for that. I'm a trustworthy guy, you know. Everyone is always saying how trustworthy I am. When it comes to trustworthiness, I am the best. There's none better than me. Trust me." Bunyip straightened his taut red vest and raised his chest with heightened prominence.

"'Ere now," he continued, "I'll put it in writing, see. I have a treaty and everything… I won't clear any more trees and you don't have to return to this area for an entire age. True to my word."

Walken looked over the first contract she'd ever looked over before. She looked it up. And she looked it down.

Yes, it was indeed a contract. And apparently, these things are binding.

It said all the things that had been agreed on. No more clearing from Bunyip, he'll show respect, treat everyone equally, unite for the greater good of the land. All in exchange for no regular visits from Walken.

"We'll do things on your terms this once. With your fancy cursives. As a show of faith and hospitality in this magical land. I expect the same respect to be shown in everything you do in this place."

"Yes, yes, sure, sure. Will you sign then? Right here please." Bunyip licked his lips and cracked the knuckles on his pudgy right hand.

The wisps painted a marking on the paper that flowed with a spectrum of vibrant colour.

"Exxccellent," whispered Bunyip, dismissively.

Walken turned north and continued her travels, intoxicated by false promise.

The next morning, Edee left Bilyakep along the song line on the way to the neighbouring country. The gravel moved loosely under Edee's feet. Their coarse surfaces rubbed against each other like nails down a chalkboard. The sensation he felt as they ground each other rested uncomfortably in his teeth. He sang along the mapping song lines to ease this feeling.

Akikarre! Edee's mind interrupted his song.

Ahead on the trail was a wild spanned bush with scaled brown bark and small green leaves. Edee rushed towards it and grabbed at the base of one of the twigs and snapped it clean off. It began to ooze an amber sap from its severed end.

Spin it! Quicker now! Look, it's all over you, Grandmother had said to Edee the first time he picked this sweet treat. *Gather it on its end, like this.*

Edee spun the stick to match the rate of the excretion and gathered it in a small bulb. The sap hardened as the stick twirled and the bulb snowballed to the size of his thumbnail. The stem clotted its bleeding and Edee placed its end in his mouth.

Mmmm, he thought, flashing back to a time with Grandma. The lessons he once felt unimportant in his youthful impatience continued to flash to him. *I should have paid more attention.*

A small bounce in Edee's step hurried him along the path with his new lollipop in hand. An old tree— older than any others in the forest around—greeted him with it's sign.

Three stones, each a deep maroon and about the size of a fist, were lodged deeply into its bark. The trunk had grown to absorb the stones over generations. For now, however, and all the times before, it was a sign that Edee had arrived at the border of Bilyakep and Badagurra. His skin tingled with the amount of time that this tree had observed and all those who had marvelled at it before him.

Uncle would tell stories about those before and

their magic. *The unseen, he'd say. They weren't wander-*
ing spirits. Nor were they living women and men. They
flow through the line of the worlds—the undead and the
non-living. They wear a cloak of light and roam the plains
of time.

Kadachi wear 'em. Kadachi, the person in between, said
Uncle. They take a leaf, like this one 'ere. Then he puts
an opal in that leaf. He thinks then. Thinks really hard,
I imagine. About how to hide. A cloud surrounds them.
Flashes of light, deep rumbles fill the ground. They turn into
anything they want and speak all languages. Even nothing
if they wish to! They walk with the dead and play with the
living.

Edee took a few leaves for cooking and a few more
for sentimentality for his Uncle. Their smell was
pleasant in his hands; the freshly crushed eucalypt
cleared his sinuses as he inhaled a fair whiff.

Down a small trodden path away from the trail
was a natural enclave hidden behind the thick
bushes. The way was well worn, and heavy footsteps
disturbed the soil. Edee saw a gunyah, as he slowly
approached the camp. Its wooden frame tied together
with woven strands that bore the craftsmanship of
Bilyakep rested against the massive trunk of a karri
tree. A cladding of spinifex was woven through the
slats of the frame.

Edee shook the gunyah and sprinkles of dried

spinifex glided to the floor like a snowfall.

This has been here some time, Edee inferred and continued to investigate the area.

"Coo-ee?!" he cried to an empty wind. The leaves howled to him, the trees groaned and the shrubs mourned at what they had witnessed. All pleaded to Edee's deaf ear.

A woomera and short spear were propped up against the same tree. They were painted with the markings of Karlaboodja. There was a small mound of leaves that partially covered their presence. The blackened ash of the fire had scattered to the wind, leaving only a suggestion of its warmth. On the ground lay a broken shield in three distinct pieces. The blunt force necessary for shattering this shield would have been fierce. Edee's mind began to play out the story of the little girl. These large hairy beasts played in his imagination and his heart began to seep adrenaline into his veins.

Edee's stomach gurgled as it burned the last of his sugary treat. Across the light covering of earthy granules was the weaving track of a long tail and spanned footprints. The line swayed in the sand with a deeply trodden talon print at each peak of its weave. *Goanna!* Edee recognised the prints; they were unmistakable. He dropped down to a low squat and moved smoothly with the tracks. The bush ahead of him rustled. His heart rate increased. *Easy now. Slow is smooth and smooth is precise.*

Edee leapt over the bush. He honed in on the creature in his motion to land, thumbs touching at their tips and hands aggressively poised.

THERE!

The thin end of the goanna's tail slipped between Edee's fingers and scampered off through another bush. He gathered himself and sprang again for the creature, missing it entirely.

Edee rose to his feet with a scurried haste and chased after his meal on the run. He hurdled another bush, larger than the first, with ease, never once losing sight of his prey. He jumped over another shrub after seeing the goanna sprint into it.

At the peak of his jump, the goanna popped its head out of the other side of the bush. Edee landed, legs straddling either side of the lizard, plucked its head with his left hand and swiftly opened its throat with the well-sharpened stone knife in his right.

Edee rested after the chase and sat sombre for a moment at the death of the goanna. "Thank you for this," he muttered and released a sigh.

On the way back to the campsite, Edee was struck with a vicious bout of goosebumps. He felt the area he was moving through, as if he'd been there before——in a memory. Edee felt a tightness constrict his chest as a breeze raised the hairs on the back of his neck. He stopped in the middle clearing beside the camp and gently shivered with unrest.

The ground was heavy and tumultuous. A thick brown clay that had hardened in the wind and sun made the surface uneven. Scrapes linked some foot-prints together. Messy piles of mud were thrown all around and sprinkled the leaves of the bushes nearby. Edee did not remember feeling the uneven surface in his chase and now tried to replay their origin in his mind.

The bushes that surrounded the area were compressed and broken. Their limbs hung limply at the force of destruction and swayed in the wind like a ragdoll on a noose. A glint from below the dried mud caught Edee's eye. He excavated the golden object from its place and pushed aside the thick brown dirt. The earth was smudged into the gaps of the insignia, highlighting its curves and edges.

Edee had never seen such a shine or felt something as weighted as his new trinket. Its markings were intentional but held no meaning to Edee. A three-pronged emblem above two waving horizontal lines. It looked like some type of hat or marking of forest ahead. Strange to Edee, either way. He placed the object into his dilly-bag and jingled it around. The new clanging sound was nice and added a softer ring to it than the percussion of the gemstones before.

Yes. This will do nicely, Edee thought.

Tracks led away from the campsite to a path on the opposite side of the bushland. The muddy soil on both sides of the trail was heavily imprinted with toeless footprints. Their heel was rounded at the back, with a strict and resolute squared edge on the inner face. In the centre of these deep prints was a smooth, unbroken line like a crocodile's belly against the soil. They led to a path at the top of the small hill behind the camp.

The soil of the trail was beaten thick and bumpy all over like measled skin. Edee felt nauseous as he knelt to touch the prints. He returned to the camp and continued along the song lines, his new trinket adding to the melody of his jangle.

CHAPTER 8

"Ok, ok. I think I've finally got it," voiced Dom, "so what comes next?"

"Well, we're walking at the moment," replied Kenny, "and we'll walk for a little while longer."

"Yeahhh. But then what?!" huffed Dom. "I'm bored. Let's go back to the boredroom and make people sneeze, just for fun."

"The boardroom smelt of sweaty, rotten milk," cried Kojak, through a gentle gag. "I'd rather walk a bit longer."

"Well, where are we going? Can you tell me that?"

"We've got to find out what went wrong," said Kenny.

A soft breeze blew against their cloaks and cooled their feet. The gentle sound of crashing waves echoed through time.

"See, we're not far now," continued Kenny.

The ocean water rocked its deep blue against the

fading light of the sky. Waves lapped against the hard wood of a tall ship anchored a short distance off the sandy coast. It was thirty metres long with huge broad planks that forged together her white oak exterior. Hardened pine masts stretched up towards two and a half square kilometres of sturdy flax sail. Lanterns hung from the siderails and along the walls of the cabin, their soft light barely enough to pierce a shadow.

There were five men inside the cabin sitting around a thick wooden table. On top of it was a sprawled-out map, a sexton, a compass and an inkpot stabbed with stained white feather quills.

"Right then. What are we going to do with these ones…?" questioned a thin man in a starched red coat.

***

"Oh look! The beach! I love the beach!" proclaimed Dom and he raced away from the other Wulgi.

"Wait!" yelled Koko, but Dom had already joined the men in the cabin—taking form as a cannon ball in the corner.

***

Braump A thud hit the ground on the wooden floor of the cabin.

"What was that?" asked Will.

"Yeah, I heard it too," replied Patrick.

"What are you two on about?! Will you focus here? I'm sure it was nothing," snapped James.

"Go on with what you were saying, James," redirected his second in command, Zach.

"Come on then... we'd better go down," signed Kenny.

"Ohh, but do we have to? I get sea sick...," warned Kojak.

"It's not that bad. You'll be fine. We'd better catch up before he does some damage," decided Koko.

The other Wulgi joined their cannonball associate in the humid cabin. Kenny formed himself into a quill and dived into the ink pot, splashing drops onto the table. Koko took a place in the corner as a tricorn hat atop the coat rack and Kojak came in as a bowl of chunky stew perched on the side of the table.

"I did not see any structures at all. No churches, schools or hospitals, not even homes," proclaimed James.

"What dooya spose it means, Cap?" drawled Patrick.

"Well. You worship in a church, you educate in a school, you heal in a hospital and you live comfortably in a home. It would only be reasonable then to infer that they lack religion, intelligence and the capacity for medicines."

"I agree," stressed Zach firmly.

"Makes sense, I guess," concurred Patrick.

"Will you stop squirming!" said the tricorn to the bowl of stew.

"I can't help it! It's so bumpy... I... I—" replied the stew.

"Don't you do it!" interjected the quill.

"Haha! Do it!" yelled the cannonball.

"Then what're we to do with them?" asked Will.

"That's a tough one. See, I've been given very strict criteria on what we are to consider 'populace' and what does not classify as such. At the moment, all I can report back to the Crown, by their own definition, is an empty land."

"But—I don't get it—it's not empty. We've seen them ourselves. They waved at us; we even shared a laugh. You were there," implored Will.

"I understand. But we must work within these definitions. I'm not responsible for them, I just follow them. It's out of my control," responded James.

"Oh, just... move them all along," justified John, contributing for the first time on the matter.

"Well, welcome to the conversation!" piped in Will.

"I'm serious. You ever been to the colonies? I have. Wretched place. Trouble with the natives there.

Only thing these people understand is violence and savagery—so you gotta treat 'em like such," continued John.

"Now, now… we're the explorers, botanists and astronomers, not the conquerors," replied Zach.

"Yeah, well, s'my opinion anyway. You don't get nothin' from working with these people. They'll take you in for a while, sure. Then, as soon as you get comfy and expand your territory—into some of the millions of acres they own anyway—they get all uppity. Nah… deal with 'em early I say, easier for the long-haul than all this 'are they, aren't they'—whadda we do with 'em? Feed 'em, cloth 'em, teach 'em all we know? That'd take ages!"

"Are you finished?" asked James.

"Eeurgh," replied John, who slumped back into this chair.

"Please continue, sir," resumed Zach.

"It's done really. I'll report back terra nullius and the Crown can progress as they wish."

"What's religion?" asked the cannonball.

"I think they mean spirituality," replied the quill.

"It's like a club for spirituality. They make you sit and stand and touch your head, chest and shoulders."

"Oh, like aerobics?" replied the cannonball. **"I like aerobics."**

"No, not quite I don't think. I'll show you later," said the quill

"You're right, sir. There's no way we can say otherwise. I've seen enough through the telescope from the deck of the ship to see," stated Zach.

"Guys?" interrupted the stirring bowl of stew. **"It's happening."**

bleu, bleuuur, bleuuurghhh

The bowl of stew chundered its gooey slop over the hard-wooden floor.

"What the hell?!" yelled John, whose shoes now wore most of the stew. "Who left their dinner here? Who's gonna bloody clean this mess up?! Cause I'm sure bloody not."

"Oops, time to go…," said the quill.

"Ha, ha, ha, run!" laughed the cannonball.

The Wulgi returned to the time above and watched the men scurry to blame.

"Well, that went worse than I expected," exclaimed Koko.

"Yes… I don't remember it happening like that last time," Kenny recalled.

"Blegh," uttered Kojak.

"Haha, feeling better there, Mr Stew?" queried Dom.

"Shut up. Please. Their twisting words made me dizzy enough. I don't need to hear yours too," replied Kojak grumpily.

Edee had been walking, the problem of the campsite in his mind.

The scene played out repeatedly, each time a small detail changed or skewed to make more sense in his understanding. He recognised the same symbol embedded deep into the trunk of a nearby tree, signalling that he had crossed territory. Without interrupting the investigation of his imagination, Edee pulled off to the side of the path.

Edee placed his shield on the ground. He set the firestone and placed a handful of dried grass into the bowl. A calmness came over him. The calmness of ceremony.

Here he waited, fixated on the unknown. He thought of Tilda as he gazed into the gap between the wood and the flame. Memories of her swam in the soft pools of tears that collected in his eyes. Edee thought of her safety and hoped she was protecting herself against her own unknowns as she too moved forwards into destiny.

The birds chirped their evening tune in the trees above as they ushered in the night. They watched the earth rotate and set the sun behind its own shadow. Reds, purples and oranges played along the soft undercarriage of the clouds.

"Kiya, Kiya!" said a voice from beyond the scrub.

Edee snapped from his trance and turned to it.

"Kaya!" he said into the bush curtain.

A head popped out of the covering with a smile that flashed thick, healthy white teeth at Edee. They were the biggest teeth he'd ever seen, like marble pillars carved to chew.

"Come on this way, meal is about done and you'll make us miss it!" blurted the toothy grin, "Come on!! I'm not missing out because you came at a bad time. Let's move it!"

A cold had set in Badagurra country that evening like Edee had never felt before. The chilled winds tore through his clothing and skin. The sky had poured intermittently the whole time he'd been there, broken by a light blue sky that offered little warmth.

Edee had walked away from the group to marvel at the wondrous surrounds. Life sprang from the high stone walls and stretched to the top. The trees, with trunks larger than at least ten arms spans, stretched out.

The porous limestone seeped yesterday's rain from its towering ceiling. A thin sheet of ice formed from the tip of his nostril, down his larynx and sat deeply in his lungs. Edee found himself breathing through his nose as quickly as he could to gauge the full experience of its chill. He rubbed his nostrils and exhaled deeply to ease the sting.

An aromatic smoke wafted over the area that beckoned Edee. He made his way through the foliage, pushing away the branches that fanned their thin green leaves, which were as wide as Edee's palm. The smell clung to the damp air and lingered in the thin forest.

Edee broke through the covering to arrive at the camp. Off to the side was a group of women and children, both boys and girls. They were all together humming a rhythmic beat. Each took turns, in a type of question and answer, singing their improvised verse. The solo was passed around first to the left two people, they would sing their part, and then it went back one to the right, they too would sing, and it would then pass to two people to the left again.

Tied to their big toes were blades of thick grass reed woven with strands of animal hair and fur, combined with a sap resin. The other end was in their hands and they wove the materials as they sang together. When they had each made a collection of the thin rope, they repeated the process again to plait a stronger, thicker rope.

Behind them, suspended from a large wooden frame, was a masterfully made net. On the other side of the stand, it bundled in a pile that looked as though it could expand to the whole area of the camp. Its mesh gaps were precise and exact with finely woven joins that seemed unbreakable.

"They're always making them. We start in the Birak and don't get finished until the next Djeran! Imagine that," explained the escort. "Yep, got one active, one in reserve and making the next one. We're the best at it."

In the centre of the gathering was a wooden frame that stood over a blazing fire. Atop the frame, squired in a row, were a collection of goannas. The meat sizzled above the flames. A group of self-appointed chefs stood around the grill, each with a firmly protruding belly. They were all standing facing the fire with their arms folded and favouring their weight off to one side.

"Turn it now," demanded one.

"Not yet. It's not ready yet," rebutted another.

"Just flip it back later then," suggested the first.

"Flip it twice?! Have you ever cooked before?"

"I've cooked plenty. You don't know what you're doing."

"Shut it. I'm flipping once. If you want yours done like that, I'll toss it in the dirt for extra seasoning."

"Ahh, you don't know what you're doing. It's gotta be crispy! You'll ruin it if it's still raw," insisted the frustrated second man, fanning his hands dismissively. Out of the corner of his eye, he saw Edee. "Karlaboodja! Come here!!"

Edee joined the group. He wanted to jump into the smoke he was so hungry.

"Flip it once? Or over and over again, Karlaboodja? You should know," asked the first man, scratching the top mound of his gut.

"It's gotta be tender and a little raw in the middle. That's what Dad always said."

"ArghHH," repeated the second man. "You don't know what you're talking about."

The laughter faded to low tone sighs.

"You should probably flip it now," advised a third voice from the many chefs.

———————————

———————————

Later that evening, after all had shared the meal, six members of the community and Edee remained around the dwindling fire. The atmosphere of the night was calm and comfortable. These few had endured through their fatigue, for that special slow conversational rhythm at the end of the night. The party beyond the party.

A jester figure stood from the group, intoxicated by the night, and stole the ears of his audience. He clapped his hands and stomped his right foot. In one movement, he spread his arms out from his centre and slid his leg to a broader stance.

"NOW!" he yelled, prompting his freestyle story. "Hear this! Watch me! Imagine what it was. The story of our evening meal. And you guess who this is…"

He crouched down to his hands and moved on all fours gingerly, birthing an unsuspecting prey into the minds of the audience.

———

Kangaroo nibbles at the offerings of a nearby shrub. It raised its head and scratches its ear by brushing its forearm over its head.

———

The storyteller morphed himself into a human again. A hunter. His chest was pushed upwards and forwards with the confidence of a big city pigeon and the strut to match.

———

The hunter spied Kangaroo, unsuspecting and still nibbling. He lowered himself behind cover, clanging his weapon clumsily against it.

Kangaroo, alerted for a moment, inspected the area and continued to graze.

Hunter breathed deeply to calm his thumping heart. He aimed his weapon and prepared to strike. In one leap he vaulted over the log. As he came to land on the other side, a rouge branch revealed itself in his path, and struck him hard in between his legs.

———

The storyteller dropped his imaginary weapon and clutched both hands to his groin.

"OW! OW! OW!" he screamed.

The man hopped from one leg to the other, flailing about himself in pain.

———

Kangaroo looked over to Hunter, chuckled, and hopped away.

———

Their leader, Bridya, bounced her shoulders in hearty laughter.

"HEY! I got him in the end, didn't I?" pleaded Krugar, the hunter from the story.

"Gurahya, I remember you doing this! Haha! Although yours was a little better," she pointed at her companion sitting beside her and redirected her continued laughter away from the story.

"Nooo. Don't, please," begged Gurahya. "I've got stories on you too, you know!"

"Yeh? Go on, tell 'em! I'm still going to speak this one."

Bridya switched places with the brave initial story-teller and got into the starting position for her story.

"The hunter that moves with the wind, they call him," she began with a cheeky smirk. "He had keen vision and steady aim. He could strike like a snake with equal precision. But he had one weakness."

Bridya poised her character as he was aiming at the same goanna still lingering in the imagination of the audience.

———————

The Windy Hunter moved with a low gravity crouch silently. His toes moved the earth that cascaded over his sprawled digits. Ready, with spear held firmly beside his ear, Gurahya exclaimed a triumphant groan.

———————

Bridya crouched as her character and let loose a tremendous fart. It rested on the confronted silence of her crowd.

———————

Goanna ran off into the bushes, to fresh-aired safety.

———————

At once, they erupted into convulsive laughter. They all clutched their sides and covered their eyes as tears streamed down their faces. They struggled for breath and heaved from their chests. All except Gurahya, who sat, arms folded, staring at Bridya with an unimpressed glare.

"Ha, aha, haha… ahhh," their exhausted sigh tapered out, and with it, the evening.

"Bridya…," whispered a gentle voice from outside the circle. The group fell silent with the weight of the entry.

"Yes, Kali. Come, please," Bridya invited Kali, Badagurra's healer, to speak.

"Brethya's condition worsens. His skin bubbles in patches that continue to spread. A heavy cough and boiling fever rattles him in his rest. Davura shows the early signs too, with yellowing crust around his lips. We'll all sleep and check them both again," reported Kali.

"Thank you, Kali. Please come get me if you need me to watch over the patients through the night."

"Yes, Aunty," Kali reassured her, returning to the open shelter that housed the sick hunters.

The mood in the group had sobered with the news.

"What is it, Bridya. What do we know?" asked an inquisitive bystander.

"We don't know. They had just come back from their travels from the east. Little cough is all they had. They were a bit cold. But it is cold. So, nothing out of the ordinary. Then the cough started getting bad. Really deep in the chest. Sounds wet too."

"Stop… that's enough," interrupted the queasy questioner. "I get it. They're sick."

"Proper sick too. More than I've ever seen. They've got, like, sores on their skin, too," contributed another bystander.

"There's a story 'bout sickness," imparted Marra, the oldest woman in the group. "Story of a creature. Snarly and mean. Those who told it to me said it came in a dream. This creature, he roams. He roams lost of a home—lost of community. So, he makes his own, the sad beast. No one wants to be with him, you see. They are already doing things their own way in the spirit." Marra changed her voice.

"*'Come innn,' the beast says. 'Come innn, I'm the only one to care for you. The mother is misguiding your ways. I have better food. Better humpies. Better carrrreee.'*"

When the beast spoke, her voice rode out to a slithering gurgle from the back of her throat.

"So, he catches a few spirits. Keeps them in. And feels good for a bit. But that loneliness starts to build again. Worse this time, too. *'Ohhhh. More. I neeeeedd more.'* So, he went out. And caught more this time, too. That camp starts to grow. Beast gets stronger too with every spirit he captures in his system. No more pain in that beast. He stretches his chest wide and screams, *'FEAR ME!'* This must have shaken his memory. That beast starts to think that the spirits outside his camp are the ones who're lost, not him. *'I must guide them! They must be in my camp!!! It's the only place they're safe.'"*

"The spirit's trapped. They cough. Their noses leak. They have sores, like you say. They sick. Like our two men sick. That's what my Grandmother said in her future dreaming. That what it is."

Edee, who'd been sitting as still as an ornament as the Badagurra country had their discussion, cleared his throat gently. He rubbed his palms against his thighs back and forth and stood to quietly remove himself from the gathering.

"You there," inquired Jorra to Edee, who'd been listening quietly amongst the group. "We might need your help. You ever hunted duck?"

"Me?" Edee turned. "No, never."

"What do you mean, no? You're telling me you've never even caught one duck?" continued Jorra.

"Never hunted them, anyways. Watched them in the sky plenty."

"You've never… really?" Jorra paused and stared

at the ground, imagining a life absent of ducks. "Anyway, it's easy. We just need the numbers. You'll see tomorrow, anyway. See you then!"

Edee understood the dismissive cue and continued back to his guest humpy. A tickle in his throat flashed the story of the sickness in his mind. Oh no… he thought, seduced by a late-night hypochondria.

———

Edee woke up after a sleep so deep he did not even remember closing his eyes. The bustle of the chores indicated to him that it was late into the morning. The warming sun had defrosted the cold air of the night.

He was late and hurried to meet with Jorra and the other hunters. Violent wheezing was coming from the medical shelter where Kali had been treating the patients. He saw Jorra standing by there and rushed over.

"Jor—" Edee stopped on a breath.

On the ground lay the corpse of Brethya. His skin was bumpy with a field of bulbous sores. The whites of his eyes were tinged with a poisoned yellow, his mouth blistered with boils. A terror rested in his face, a terrible unknowing of the horror that simmered within.

Davura had gone into a sleep during the night,

from which he had yet to wake. His skin had begun to present the same protrusions that trickled over his entire body. A faint cough fluttered his lips and jumped his chest with a jolt.

"Come," beckoned Jorra to the hunting party, "we should clear this area in case the sickness jumps to us as well. Edee, get those nets over there."

Jorra turned back into the shelter and said to Kali, "We will mourn for him tonight, after the hunt. Continue your treatments of Davura, until we learn what else can be done."

—————————

The hunt began later that day at the shores of the river. Each side of the river was a line of thick trunked karri trees. The white of their fresh bark bounced the sun back into Edee's eyes and he lifted his forearm to shade its rays. He squinted his eyes and looked up to the tall trees.

"Ok. We'll set up here," commanded Jorra. "Edee, you're with me. You and I are going to run beside the river to set the boundaries on either side. When they break for flight, throw your arms out and scream at them."

"Got it," replied Edee.

"You two," continued Jorra "Take the reeds and get in position behind the raft from below the water. Hold your nose with one hand and hold the hollow tube with the other. Remember, you must move slowly. Step firmly against the current. We'll all be waiting on your cue. Right, everyone else, you know your roles. Let's get to it!"

The group of eight split into four parties of two and took up their stations. Three of them, including Jorra, went further upstream to cross without disturbing the flock that was expected to pass later in the day.

The two divers walked in the opposite direction in search of their reeds for the operation. One of them picked up a collection of sticks and large pieces of bark and walked into the water. He dived down and drove one end of the markers into the soft sands of the riverbank. His head popped up, he shook off the water and re-joined his partner.

"Well, up I go then, ha-ha," beamed Gurahya as he wiped the sand from the soles of his feet.

He walked up to the tall karri tree and slapped it hard with the soft flesh of his palm. Then, with one soft pounce from his calf, he quickly shuffled himself up the trunk. The soles of his feet pressed against opposing sides and launched him to the next checkpoint. He tightly hugged the tree and repositioned his feet for another thrust.

About half way up the tree was a platform that collared the trunk. Gurahya hopped up onto its sturdy base, supported by the thick branches, and looked back down to Edee, dangling his legs over the side.

"Uu-huuu," waved Gurahya from the platform.

In his hand he held a rope that led back down the tree on the waterside. Attached to it was a great bundled up mesh netting that stretched from one side of the river to the other, hidden under the water. He gave it a few tugs to make sure it was flowing nicely on his end. A gentle ripple marched up the surface of the river.

The other three had made it to the other side. One of them hopped up a tree, even quicker than his counterpart. When he was at the top, he gave a small fist pump and tested his rope attached to the woven net.

The last pair that were stationed either side with Jorra or Edee held three boomerangs, each with different sized holes bored in their ends. One of the men used the long-curved weapon to scratch his back while they waited.

The sun of the day had risen higher in the sky. Gurahya, still stationed in the platform in the karri tree, was slumped over in his own lethargy. He nodded his chin towards his chest as he flirted with slumber and jolted himself awake, nearly falling from the tree.

"Whoaa! Ahh, oh!" yelled Gurahya.

Jorra gave a stern look and a clear signal that he needed to be quiet.

"What is it?" Edee forcefully threw a whisper up to Gurahya.

"Nothing… thought I was falling. It's nothing," replied Gurahya.

From across the other side, Jorra clicked his tongue through his teeth and chirped for the attention of the others.

There they are! thought Edee.

A large raft of ducks paddled up the river towards the six waiting men. Two tubed reeds followed behind at a steady pace as to not disturb the water. The ducks floated by, unawares of the ambush ahead, and chattered amongst themselves.

The divers felt the sticks and bark at their feet, and they knew they were in range. One of the divers reached out his hand in search for his partner. They joined hands to coordinate the trigger and pounced on their targets.

The two with the boomerangs threw them at each other across the river. As the weapons turned, they roared in the air that ripped through the bored holes. Their wooden wings flapped the sound of the eagle hawk, which kept the ducks low to the water. The men exchanged tools like lethal jugglers, concentrating on accuracy.

Jorra and Edee matched the pace of the ducks and ran beside them on the shore. Edee waved his arms wildly and made unrehearsed noises he hadn't been sure he could make. He giggled as he ran, waving his arms and legs all about.

Gurahya and his partner pulled hard on their ropes and raised the net into the path of the ducks. They hit the net one by one, tangling in the small woven gaps. The net was lowered into the water as the divers and Jorra jumped in to hold it below the water.

Edee and the two throwers jumped in after them to recover the bodies. They stacked them on the shore and enjoyed the calm ripples of the river pass by.

"Gurahya, why do you get to go up the platform?" asked Edee.

"Cause I'm the best climber," he boasted.

"No way. He shot up there like he was running," rebutted Edee, pointing at Gurahya's partner. "You climbed it like a fish. You'd make a better diver, for sure."

"Well he can't be a diver," chortled Jorra, "he can't hold his breath out both ends at one time! That's impossible for him."

CHAPTER 9

It was time for Edee to leave Badagurra and its calming river streams. Their waters rushing over the rocks shone a white noise around its banks. The sound was calming and had a way of resting comfortably in the back of your neck, like the warm palm of a lover.

Edee packed his swag with a vacant mind. A type of organic routine had developed within him and evolved into ritual.

The kangaroo skin was laid out on the ground, tanned side down. He piled in his things on the centre of the outstretched sheet. First, the ever-handy paperbark then, inside that, a sharpened stone and rigid curved stick for sparking fire.

"Edee…," came a soft voice from behind his back.

Edee turned to see a woman whose short height and skinny frame made her easy to look over. She was holding a delicately painted rod, about as long and wide as her forearm.

"I'm Liara of Katakonda." She extended her arms with the rod in hand. "I have a message for Kulanda, my sister."

Edee looked over the delicate tracings, thinking of his own wobbly and clumsy outlines. "Who is this?"

"That's Kwenda ; that's my totem," replied Liara. "Tell them, I still remember their faces. And Goolra, tell him I still remember his stupid laugh… and that I miss them…"

Liara's voice faded in a dull sadness.

"Of course, Liara. Of course, I will." Edee gently took the message from her open palms with great care and placed it with his belongings in his unwrapped swag. Once all these things were neatly stacked, Edee took each corner of the skin and met them in the middle. He bundled them together and tied them securely with the reed woven rope, attaching it to the end of his spear.

"How will you get it back?"

"Haha, it doesn't matter. I like painting them fresh each time. Each stroke allows me to sit and talk in memory with my family. I think of them often."

Liara let slip an emotional sigh and reactively covered her mouth with her hands.

Edee wrapped his swag and hoisted it over his shoulder.

———————

———————

The same rustling of the water comforted his journey as he travelled along the path towards Katakonda.

Danger comes in many forms. Large beasts roam here and there, sure—but you can see and hear them coming. The fiercest of those are the ones who creep. Those critters so small yet they hit the hardest. Single bite and death, from a culprit the size of your smallest fingernail.

Even from above, danger lurking. Those that swoop can do damage as well. Again, none so fierce as the smallest swooper.

Chitty chitty!

The sharp beak of a bird clipped Edee's ear as it flew past.

"Ah! My ear!!" Edee responded in a panic, frantically searching around the skies for his attacker.

Chitty chitty, KA!

The bird swooped again. This time it landed and fronted Edee on the path he had been singing. Edee looked at the bird with his face scrunched in confusion, still clutching his pecked ear.

Chitty chitty!!! The bird took a hop closer to Edee, waving its stiff fanned tail from side to side.

It wasn't even as big as a clenched fist and did not

stand taller than the ankle, but that did not matter to the confident miniature. It had battled larger beasts than Edee and fought greater battles than you or I could imagine—so there was no challenge in dismembering the prey he saw before him.

Edee raised both of his palms facing outward from his chest.

"Whoa, little guy. I'm just passing through. I don't need nothing from you. I'm just going to go on around ya here." Edee went to move left.

Chitty chitty, KA!!! The bird hopped to its right. Its eyes squinted with determination.

"Ok, ok." Edee moved to his right.

Chitty...

The bird had allowed it, this one time. Its tail wagged defiantly, for he knew that the day was his to claim. Another victory for the mighty chitty chitty.

____

____

BANG

A tremendous noise clapped through the trees and echoed in Edee's ears. He crouched down and looked around him frantically. It was a sound he'd never heard, a confusing thunder on another otherwise clear day. He quickly gathered himself and took cover with his spear behind a fallen tree. The spear was aimed towards the direction of the assaulting sound.

BANG, BANG, BANG, BANG

The sound rang through the valley, louder and closer than before. Edee was terrified, pointing his spear at different spots in the foliage in front of him. He could feel a gentle rumble in the ground after the series of explosions.

Edee defended his position until early dusk painted the sky above. He moved cautiously towards the meeting point.

———

Edee had arrived at the meeting place for Katakonda invitation. A configuration of stones, deeply embedded into the suffocating bark of a marri tree, let him know that it was okay to set up his fire.

Edee put his shield on the ground, now covered in a light blackened ash, and placed the prod where it goes. He set the firestone and placed a handful of dried grass into the bowl. A calmness came over him. The calmness of ceremony. Friction brought out the fire behind a single strand of wafting smoke.

The rocks that bordered the fire began to steam as their moisture lifted to the heat and was carried away with the smoke.

Edee took some pieces of duck meat out of a salted leaf wrap and placed it on the hot rocks. He poked at them with a cleaned stick and made sure they faced the flame evenly. The smell of dinner quickly distracted him from how long it was taking for his escort to arrive and he focused on the plump meal ahead.

————————————

Some time had passed into the night and yet Edee still sat alone by the fire. Its embers crackled into the cool breeze and its flames licked inside Edee's heavy eyelids.

He was half asleep and peeked at his surroundings through blurred vision. The clouds reflected a collection of reds and oranges in the sky. The colours danced brightly. Edee thought for a moment that it was dawn breaking but quickly surrendered to his comfort.

The weight of it—the long day that had been and his aching feet—it all rested on his eyelids. They slowly fell to meet each other and close the lashed veil over their eyes.

POP rang out from the fire and Edee, heavy eyed, was jolted awake, but only for a second. The flames stroked his mind back to its slumber. And before Edee was aware, he has slipped into unconsciousness with a full belly by the warmth of the fire.

The trees shone brighter and brighter into the night while Edee slept. They joined the clouds and watched on at the devastation below.

———————

It was his own snoring that woke him up that morning.

"Urghh, huh, hmm?" Edee's mouth smacked against a dry tongue as he was introduced to a new day.

The fire had left a pile of white ash, whose warmth still emanated from the remains. There it waited.

The world began to make itself clear to the new day. Edee wiped at his eyes and yawned deeply, scratching his bare stomach as he arched his back to the sun.

Water first, he thought to himself. The stream nearby babbled and called to his thirst. You could almost hear how fresh it was. It was like pouring a liquid crystal over glass, the two marrying in a partnership of clarity.

Edee splashed his face with the water. He cupped it and rinsed under his arms and over his back.

"Whoo!!!" he exclaimed as the cool water ran down his back, shocking him out of his drowsy state. He cupped another handful and slurped it down quick as a flash.

There was a shuffling coming from up the bank of the river. Edee rushed out of the water, flailing and splashing about in an attempt to find his footing in the soft bed of the river.

The shuffling was slow and progressed in an even beat.

schhh,t one foot drags.

schhh,t and the other follows.

Her left arm dangled aimlessly from her body, flopping to the force of her shuffling movement. Her coverings were torn and her flesh was abraded. Thin clumps of long hair clung to her skull in a field of a ravaged and torn scalp. Tears glazed her cheeks, mixing with blood and snot to create a mask of significant trauma.

Edee opened his mouth to speak and could only let out a small crackle from his throat, stunned as he watched her.

The zombie-like wanderer fell to the ground like a lump of meat released from the butcher's hoist. She laid in a collection of her own flesh and bones and sobbed an exhausted cry. Edee rushed over to her and reached her in what seemed like a blink.

"Aunty! Aunty! What has happened, Aunty?!" Edee pleaded for information to lighten his confusion.

Her bottom lip flapped in and out with her heavy sobs. A hole had been ripped through her left shoulder, clean through each side. Fragmented bone splintered her torn flesh.

"AUNTY!" Edee struggled to get her attention. "Please Aunty!"

His voice squeaked in the panic and offered a swift reminder he was still more a child than adult. Edee could not recall any instruction from Grandfather or Mother for this. The smell of the charred flesh sat in his stomach and tickled the muscles deep in his throat. It felt like an age had passed before she responded, trapped in fear, his mind absent of a solution.

"No more," mumbled Aunty, as she tacked the words to each exhale. "No more. No more. All gone. No more."

Edee picked up the battered woman and slumped her over his shoulder.

One step at a time, he thought. *That's all I can do.*

He led with his left foot and followed with his right. The combined weight of Edee and his passenger sunk him deep into the soft soil below. Aunty cried a dull huff over his shoulder, dampened by the shock of her wound.

A horrible smell greeted them at the borders of Katakonda. A combination of singed hair and melted flesh. The humpies were now blackened, charred remains. There were stumps of original structures still in place.

Bodies were littered in the ash. A few survivors tinkered with what they could in the community around them. Each one lost in total devastation.

CHAPTER 10

Walken was happy and sailing through the land. She was skating eastward on a river, gliding swiftly from the sides of each bank. Easy to the left and easy again to the right. Nothing could disturb her.

She flipped onto her back and slid over the surface of the water. She could feel it grip her as she kissed against it just slightly. All things parted for her and longed for her touch.

The wisps swam in the water as well and played beneath Walken as they moved.

"You're it," squealed Mirda to Wooyan, then raced ahead of the pack.

"Nuh-uhh, it was Viola," giggled Wooyan, who chased anyway.

"Surrree?" questioned Nodjam. "I reckon it was Kawa!"

"Yoorda is it! Yoorda is it!" they all yelled.

Their colour leaked from them as they played in the water. A long trail of a spectrum of colour traced itself upstream and nourished the water. They laughed with an excited quiver while they moved about like children in a playground.

SMASH

A tremendous thud shook through Walken's core and compressed her like a slinky. She felt the force rock through her entire being and it rattled her from top to tail. The heavy stone wall cracked and shook debris from its top.

"DAMN!" Walken yelled in pain. "What. is. this...?"

She had never been hit before. The pain rested inside her like an unwanted guest. It settled in her head and radiated down to her entire body like an electric current.

The solid grey wall stretched for the sky and its top scraped the clouds. It was a structure so thick and dense that it absorbed any sound that hit it. The river sang its dull song against its surface, but the concrete silenced its flat tune. It was built to buckle for nothing and commanded the landscape absolutely.

On the other side, beyond the cold, rigid corners of the assaulting structure, was a vast pool of water.

"What? This is all meant to be river!" cried Walken. She turned to her wisps and asserted, "Not a lake. A lake does not fit here. It's trapped! It must move. It can't be still. You can't just cut off an entire river! … Can you?"

The pooled water swayed in the breeze, lost in stagnation from a home of free running flow. Algae had developed on the surface of the reservoirs all around the edge. Its green sludge bobbed with the slight waves that swayed the mass. The water was festering with its new sedentary state.

Walken dived into the water, which sent a series of expanding ripples over the surface. Her touch shook the algae that dissolved into the created waves. She broke through the water to fly above once more. She spotted a pattern on the top of the large grey dam, brown freckles from end to end.

"Those muddy footprints!" she fumed.

"THAT BLOODY BUNYIP!"

The devastation to Katakonda was immense. Edee carried Aunty through the destruction towards a small clearing so she could rest. Black soot had painted the surrounding trees and canopy above. He placed Aunty on the cleared mat so she could recover.

Stumps of shelters still leaked a soft smoke into the air, mixing with the aroma of melted flesh and charred hair. The smell sat in Edee's stomach and revolted his organs from within. He vomited immediately and with force.

None of the people around paid him any attention. Misery rested in their faces. They each wandered the remains of their home, adjusting to the devastation. Nobody was talking. They shuffled along, tending to what they could to restore what once was.

Edee moved away from the stench. He walked to the base of the giant waterfall. Its flow shaved over the blunt rocks as it had done since the beginning of its time, which was what had formed the cliff face.

A large barren shore funnelled the gentle flow of water to create a narrow valley between the banks of the river.

A curious girl, about Edee's age, confidently sat down next to him, jolting him from his dreaming.

"What's your name?" she asked boldly. "They call me Kulanda."

"Edee," said he, rubbing his chest with an open palm. "I'm sorry… for what happened."

Edee sat with Kulanda by the base of the waterfall that trickled slow tears down its face.

"Can—Can I ask what happened? What you saw?" asked Edee.

And Kulanda began to tell him of yesterday.

<hr>

The cockatoos chattered in the trees as they waited for the sun to set in the late afternoon. Two of the Katakonda men were walking out away from the central part of the camp.

A rumble filled the earth as the invaders approached, like nothing the two had felt before. They could feel its beat in their feet. The stampede was gaining in pace. An orange hue painted the clouds and quickly faded to a deep purple as the wind became colder. The men ran back to the camp, signalling to others to defend Katakonda.

A hurried pace sprang over the people who raced to their positions. The women gathered the children with the assistance of the older members and retreated to a cave behind the curtain of the waterfall.

The remaining men took up weapons and spread to various strategic defences through the camp. A row of four arched themselves at the point of entry, with a row of six behind them and the rest scattered for range attack.

Edee looked up, interrupting the imagery of the story, to look for the cavern Kulanda described. She pointed to it, beyond the curtain of the stream.

"I don't see it," squinted Edee.

"That's the point!" she replied. Kulanda shuffled over to Edee and pointed over his shoulder and directed his eyeline. "There. Look carefully, you'll see it through the breaks in the water."

"Oh yeah, Tilda, now I see it!"

"Tilda?" asked Kulanda

"What's that?" uttered Edee, confused.

"You said, 'Tilda'."

"Oh, did I? I'm sorry, Kulanda."

"Who is she?"

"She's my… well, I suppose it doesn't matter now."

The cavern peeked itself from behind the water to greet Edee.

Kulanda continued with her story as they walked to the waterfall.

The ground continued to rumble with a triumphant and purposeful beat. The front line stood strong with spears extended towards the noise and shields ready.

Into view came three large beasts topped with ghoulish men, their skin was sick looking and thin. It slopped to their bodies like paperbark loosely flaked from its trunk. Their bodies were wrapped in worn blue rags, stained with mud and dark red crusted traces of previous encounters. They galloped into the camp without invitation and stopped immediately in front of the front-line defenders.

The four defending men were shouting, with spears poised ready to launch. The men on the horses removed their pistols promptly in response to the poised spears. Both sides trembled with fear of the unknown other. An uncomfortable smell filled the tense and silent air.

"EENUFF!" snarled a ghastly voice. The atmosphere settled and chests continued to pump heavily with adrenaline on both sides of the encounter.

From behind the cover of the foliage emerged a fourth horse, larger than the others, topped with the fattest man any of the defenders had ever seen. His skin seeped out the gaps between the gold buttons of his scarlet coat. Its cuffs were frayed and faded. The horse's heavy footsteps were coupled with the chinking of a thick chain, shackled to a sturdy iron collar.

The man looked at them from beneath his brimmed leather hat; his eyes were dimmed with darkness, vacant of life. By his side was a beaten and bruised man, shackled at his wrists, his ankles in iron collars and a steel chain leash around his neck. The long curly hair of the captive hung sadly by his shoulders, matted in days old mud and blood.

The prisoner was skinny and hunched over himself as he shuffled alongside the convoy in his oppressing chains. A small scar rested on his face from a life before. The rider dismounted from his saddle, his weight causing an unforgiving squelch on the muddied ground below.

"Come, boy," demanded the man, yanking on his metal linked leash. "Is this the one? Is this the place? Where is the jewel, boy, go on? There's a good fella."

The chained man's face was swollen with purple bruises. His left eye was puffed completely shut. There were small circular burns all over his skin, raised and scabbed. They were filled with dirt and misery. Two tracks of blood trailed from his nostrils and over his upper lip, crusted over with time unattended.

"I am not from here. This is not my home." The words fell out of the tortured man's mouth and slopped lazily onto the ground below. "I don't know. I don't know these people." And he dropped to his knees with exhaustion.

"There's nothing here," reported Captain Wilmore, the fat horseman, to his troopers and he removed his pistol from its holster. "Take the chains, we need them for later," he continued.

After one of his troopers had removed the chains, he said casually, "Ah well, maybe next one." He kissed the lips of his pistol to the back of the prisoner's head.

BANG

A single pellet entered his skull and passed through his brain, taking with it the last of his suffering. The prisoner's body slumped to the ground unceremoniously.

The surrounding defenders became panicked. They looked at one another with wide gazes, their hearts pumping heavily. One of the front-line reached for his spear and pointed it at Wilmore.

"Aye aye aye!!! WHATCHAS DOIN' THERE?!" queried one of the troopers, frightened by the unexpected reaction.

"Oh shit! He's comin' straight for us!" screamed another, his voice breaking in a high pitch midstream.

BANG, BANG, BANG, BANG*

He had murdered three defenders before a second thought could interrupt. The other troopers opened fire on the spectators.

"Get back!"

BANG, BANG, BANG*

"Show me your hands!" he yelled at the women.

BANG, BANG*

At the end of the battle, five men of the country had been captured and restrained in the middle of the camp.

"Burn it! Burn the whole goddamn place down! Savages!" snapped Wilmore, getting back on his horse with a ragged breath escaping his blubbery cheeks. "Burn it in front of them and make them watch it."

He turned his steed into the bushes from where the gang had come and rode away quickly.

———

The two moved away from the waterfall and back into the central clearing of the camp. Kulanda showed Edee the prisoner's body, which was slumped in the same place it had been since his execution. Deep cuts carve his wrists, ankles and neck from the rubbing of the coarse shackles. His left hand looked shattered and there were cratered lashes riddled over his back.

That's my dad… lying dead on the ground.

Edee rushed to his dad and began to clean the soot, dirt and leaves from his body. He frantically cleaned and rubbed his father with a distant hope he would revive. The bullet hole sat just above his right eye. It was an image that would burn into Edee's psyche. He folded his father's arms over his chest and cradled him in his arms.

"We could do nothing but watch from behind the blurred curtain that veiled us in the rocks," Kulanda whispered, finishing her recollection there. She tried to quickly change topics, but Edee did not hear anything over the deafening flow of blood through his ears, like furious ocean waves.

———

Kulanda found Edee again later that day.

"Can you go to the mouth of the lake on top of the cliff and get some fish? We have too much to do here and can use the help."

Edee obliged without much thought and headed up the steep hill towards the top of the waterfall. His feet bled against the pinching loose rocks with each step but that went unnoticed.

Each step was difficult and it seemed that, each time Edee pushed his foot to hoist himself upwards, he slid down its face a little more. Soon he found a natural rhythm with which to move against the organic steps of the incline. Then, just when he felt comfortable, like he had it together, he slipped again.

Yet up the slope he continued, towards calming isolation. As he went, Edee remembered some time with Grandfather, back when Edee was still called Ted.

———

A fishing spear needs to be slender, Grandfather had explained as the two were walking through a collection of wooden lengths.

Ah! This one, definitely. Now we need to make one end pointy, that's the secret with a spear, joked Grandfather.

Grandfather and Ted were standing in a clearing near Karlaboodja. It was a field that they were using as a lake for the lesson ahead.

Now that it's sharp, it's important to focus on stance, continued Grandfather. *It's a lot different to hunting kangaroo or emu. The water can play tricks on you. It can tell you the fish is here when it isn't there at all. The water tricks your eyes, so you have to trick them too. Aim a finger length above where the water tells you the fish is. Remember that it is lying and trying to conceal itself from you. Then, when you are propped up with your arm ready, you throw!*

Grandfather brought his elbow to his knee as he leant well into his throw, launching his spear with a grunt firmly into the imaginary fish swimming in the earth.

Edee had fashioned and sharpened his spear. He stood waist deep in the body of water at the top of the cliff.

A brave fish approached him, lost from its school. Edee positioned his arm at the ready and let loose! And missed.

Reeling in his missile using its attached vine, Edee

remembered what Grandfather had taught him about the tricks that water plays.

Edee saw where the water projected the fish and adjusted for the kill shot. Again, with raised arm, Edee threw the spear, hitting his target through the side. He celebrated wildly with his speared fish, about the size of his palm, as he flailed his kill about in triumph. All the while scaring away the remaining fish with his excessive splashing.

Kulanda arrived at the top of the cliff, concerned at the amount of time that had passed. Edee stood confidently and puffed his chest with pride in his catch.

"Why are you using a spear to fish?" she asked, with her face scrunched in disbelief.

"What do you mean? This is the only way..." replied Edee.

Kulanda laughed and without saying a word walked over to the edge of the cliff where the water flowed over the fall.

"Be careful!" shouted Edee, who stood on the shore dripping wet with his limp spear.

Kulanda crouched by the edge and reached amongst the white water. She stood clutching two wooden cages sectioned with twig bars. Having a closer look, Edee noticed a row of firmly lodged branches into the edge of the cliff from where the cages had been pulled. They were spaced apart purposefully so that, while the smaller fish could swim through to continue to fatten themselves, the larger fish could not and were trapped by the force of the flowing water into the cages, making for easy gathering.

Kulanda laughed at Edee standing on the shore and walked over to him with her haul.

"Here, put that down and carry this," Kulanda tittered about Edee's undersized catch and handed him a crate full of decent sized fish.

The two walked down the steep hill to the camp.

A confession broke from Kulanda on the walk back.

"My people are worried," revealed Kulanda. "The waterways continue to die and it's becoming more noticeable each day. The water is our life force, it's our soul. We bleed this water in our veins and blow this wind from our lungs. We are the flow. No longer river people, we become lost."

Edee listened to Kulanda's description of the restriction of the river as a distraction from his own pain. It let him escape from one tragedy to the next.

CHAPTER 11

"I'm borrrreeeeddd…," screeched Dom. "Can we play a game?"

"What game would you like to play?" asked Kojak.

"… I guess I don't actually know any."

"What about a word game?" asked Koko.

"Can you play word games?" replied Dom.

"Sure, you can," replied Kenny, "or haven't you been paying attention?"

The four continued their walk as time played in the events below. There was a town that caught Kenny's eye. Its thick paved roads and steep blocked curbs carved a path through the land. Metal bars, paired and parallel, hung in the middle of the street under the blaring sun. Horses tapped along the hard ground hauling their stacked wooden carriages.

People lined the streets and wandered through the moving carts. Their black suits, their cotton vests, called to the rays that beat down from above and offered them a welcome home. They chattered and grumbled to each other about their pursuits and opinions among only those who'd agree. Draped in a garb of mid-distinction they sought a taste of exclusive paradise in the world they created for themselves.

"Do you smell that?" groaned Koko.

sniff, sniff

"Pwhoaa, that is foul!" remarked Kojak.

"I guess the horses have to go somewhere…," said Kenny.

"But… it's… everywhere…," protested Dom with a grimace.

The buildings were bumpy on the bottom with sharp chiselled edges on the top, like a sandcastle on a sloppy foundation. A chequered pattern etched the harsh surface of the wall, all enclosed by a thick coat of white paint tinged yellow with pollution.

Inside one of the heavy stone buildings was a meeting of some well-dressed men with bald heads and extravagant facial hair.

"Ooo, I wonder what they're talking about?" thought Dom as he dived straight for the scene.

The Wulgi leapt down into the room, each one changing their form as they landed. Kenny became a creaky wooden chair, positioned at the head of the table. Kojak hung from the ceiling amongst the shards of the chandelier. Koko took his place on the long table under the window as an empty silver platter and Dom sat beside him as a small bowl of strawberry jam.

Five men sat around the large wooden table making small talk as they waited for the formalities to begin. They each fanned themselves as they slumped in their chairs, suffocating in their tight coats. The starched collars that clung to their shirts rigidly held their necks strong, pointing their noses to the sky.

"Ahhh, Governor, how are those lights warming your streets?" asked the 2nd Lamington of his name.

"Yes, indeed Baron Lamington, well indeed. We've just had the new street lights put in. They're electric, you see. I would swear that the illumination they omit to be ten-fold that of the burning lantern," replied the 2nd Baron.

"Bit behind in the times, are you? What took so long, I wonder?"

"Yes. Well. A bit of trouble, you see. But that's all handled now. There shouldn't be any more troubles, we packed them up and moved them on."

"I say, have you been home recently?" asked the First Earl.

"Oh no, far too sea sick, I'm afraid," replied the 2nd Baron. "I see myself staying here until the end of my days now."

"Pardon me gentlemen, but if we may move onto

the matters at hand," interrupted the 2nd Lamington.

"Right you are. I think we must ask ourselves, here, today, what type of country we're after exactly. What type of country we will create for the people?" questioned the 7th Earl without prompt.

"I have some statistics here for us to consider," continued the First Earl, shuffling through his paper. "Ah yes, we've got a seventy seven to twenty three percentage split between homeborn and foreign born; in total just under four million people."

"Hmmm. Yes. And what of the native problem on the mainland?" said the 14th Viscount.

"They are all called Earl or Baron?" asked the creaky chair.

"Yeah, that's confusing... they all look so uncomfortable," said the silver platter.

"Lamington," interrupted the strawberry jam.

"What?" asked the chandelier.

"Lllaaahhhmmmmington", repeated the jam. **"Ha-ha, that is so fun to say... Lamington. I should like to meet him."**

The first Earl shuffled into his papers once again, foraging for the right numbers. His palms were sweaty from the humidity in the room. The five men perspired in their suits and basked in their hot air as they tossed it at one another from across the room.

"It says… says here that there's only some four hundred thousand. That's only, approximately," the Earl raised one of his eyebrows and stared at the plastered decor mouldings that laced the ceiling. "That's only two percent."

"Two percent?! It feels like they're everywhere…," snapped the 14th Viscount. "That type of decline is extinction type numbers… poor things are dying out anyway."

"Why is their hair so thin?" asked the jam. "They look like they've outgrown their skin but haven't shed."

"That's assuming we were able to survey them all," speculated the First Earl. "How far out of the settlements do you really think our statisticians went. Not to mention most of them are illiterate."

"That is true. The poor devils. Well, there's always something better, as the good book says. Even we have a long way still of ascension in the eyes of the Lord," postulated the seventh Earl. "It is our civil duty, as the superior beings open to the right-ways, to lift others into civility as we, too, rise towards His Grace."

"This is not good," groaned the creaky chair. **"This is not good at all."**

"There are two schools of thought really. That way, with your thoughts and prayers, and the right way," stated the 14th Viscount from the southern island. "And the right way is to stop this nonsense discussion over the wellbeing of the wildlife. We've got a country to form. Where is he?! I'm not sure why we have to always wait for someone like him. He should be serving us lunch, like he was born to do."

The door latch clicked as it surrendered to the turning handle. Through its opening strode Big Johnny. His muscular frame was that of a polar explorer with a thick beard and stern look of determination. He wore a lose fitting suit that was not pressed, instead it hung from him, lazily swaying as he walked.

"Ooo, look at that one! He's wild," giggled the jam.

"He looks tired. Like he could use a good nap," chuckled the chandelier.

"Sorry I'm late, fellas," announced Big Johnny, who flashed a look at the 14th Viscount. "As the only one here who actually does his own work, I'm sure you'll accommodate my delays."

"We were just about to start, John," said the First Earl, pointing to a chair on the long side of the table, "please sit."

John looked at the chair and then around to the

others. He strode headfast towards the head of the table, pulled out the chair and surrendered his tremendous weight into its frame.

"No, no, no, no! Arrrghhh!!!," the chair screamed.

"**Shhh, quiet down,**" hushed the chandelier.

"**Hahaha,**" sniggered the jam.

"**You come and hold him then!**" protested the chair.

"Gentlemen, we have to come to an agreement that suits all parties, both economically and socially," announced the First Earl.

"Yes, well. The first thing I'd like to address is, what are we going to do about the trains?" asserted the 2nd Lamington. "How are we expected to have a national network when we've each chosen different gauges for our rail carts. As we have the largest need for a functional railway, it should be our gauge that is used as the national standard."

"That's convenient, isn't it," piped in the 7th Earl. "You mean to tell me, with the largest network of railways in this country, that I have to re-lay all my lines? You've got to be joking."

"Doesn't bother me," dismissed the 14th Viscount.

"Excuse me fellas, you've still got a lotta convincing to do on my end to get me to join this little boy's club His Majesty is putting together. Quite frankly, I'm not sure we need to fund some suits out east. So, you can spend our money on what? To fill your tables with the working of the people? How much did that silver platter to serve your tea cost?" inquired John, pointing to the silver platter on the long table against the wall.

"It's absolutely essential that we make a nation, John, for the good of the people," proclaimed the First Earl, "before they grow a perception that we, their mother country, are the foreign powers. No, we will not have that again. There needs to be a nation formed early so we can still control its development. We need a country that the people can rally behind. One that stands for equality of opportunity, religion and governance."

"And how do we do that?" asked 2nd Lamington.

"Well. We'll need a white policy, obviously. To distinguish whom it is exactly are that come to our newfoundland," contended the First Earl.

"I believe it's 'who' in that context" corrected the 2nd Lamington.

"What?" replied the First Earl

"Yes, who is definitely correct – I think."

"Anyway, and how do you pay for all this? With our resources…?" scoffed John.

"No, with our resources, John," retorted the 2nd Baron, pouring himself tea from the pot. "Think of a cup of tea. The tea does not become weaker when added to the cup, but rather, it makes the drink stronger."

"**Come on,**" moaned the chandelier, "**I've heard enough. Let's go...**"

"**But they said equality for all. Didn't you hear?**" asked the jam.

"**I know what I heard, 'equality for all—*like us*', 'freedom for all—*like us*', 'opportunity for all—*all of those, like us*',**" groaned the creaky chair.

The blisters on Edee's palms cried as they rubbed against the solid wooden frame of the shovel. Its pointed end sunk deeply into the soil. The rounded body caressed a clump of the earth and moved it to one side. He repeatedly stabbed the ground, ignoring the shovel as it slipped against his fresh and bloodied skin.

It was the fourth grave Edee had dug that morning. His stomach grumbled as he pushed through the searing hunger and thirst. There was one task at hand—and it must be completed before anything else. His hands burned but were paid no attention.

Trauma severed the connection between his mind and body, suspending his thoughts for another day. He watched his arms drive the curved wood into the earth and felt his back bend to scoop the debris.

There'd be six graves dug that day by Edee alone. Another four dug by another survivor of Katakonda, Goolra. The two had not spoken a word. He kept his eyes to the ground and wore stains of dirt and tears down his cheeks. A strong pout rested in his lips and quivered in his throat.

Goolra could not bear to look around at his destroyed memories and those of his grandfather's grandfather, and his father before. Coated now in a black coat and suffocated by the white ash of the fire.

A young leader approached, self-appointed in the chaos, and barked orders at the two.

"Goolra, we need food," commanded the youngin'. "Go and kill something for us to eat. Take the traveller with y—"

"—No. I'll go alone." Goolra stood abruptly and excused himself quickly.

Edee began wrapping his hands in thick green leaves from a nearby gum to protect his blisters. The leaves cooled his wounds but resonated their sting up his arms.

"Traveller, back to it. We need these dug by light's end." The young leader, Mandi, had a role to fill also. A much more daunting one, with which came pressures before his time. He barked around the community and led from a safe distance.

"We need more wood!" he yelled at the three women chopping wood off in the bush and walked over to them with a puffed, boney, meatless chest.

Edee fell back into his half-completed grave and caught himself on his feet. The spirit of his grandmother sat on the edge of the hole, her feet dangling into the pit. An electricity ran through her arms every time the shovel dug deeper into his hands.

Grandmothers shadow's hands began to blister and the pain under Edee's reed wrapping faded. Her shadow looked at her palms and the flesh that peeled away from them—and chuckled to herself.

Her voice played in Edee's mind as he pushed through everything in him that screamed to quit.

This is the most important thing of all. Make sure that spirit makes it back. Above all else, Ted. Above all. The spirit wanders here now until it can be put to rest and become anew, Grandmother said into Edee's imagination. *We're all made of this earth. Like all things. We return to it. Our matter becomes shared and we contribute to new life. The burial puts the physical to rest and lets the spirit find peace. An undue death is the most horrific of all. Its ripples shimmer through time in this world and the world around us.*

Her spirit chuckled again. *There's a good boy.*

Edee turned suddenly with shock, but there was

nobody there. The wraps had separated as their crude knots came undone and they wore to the force of the shovel. He felt a breeze stroke the flesh of his palm and he pulled away the rags of the bandage.

His wounds were healed, skin fused and hard calluses where before had been pitted blisters. Immediately, Edee felt a wave of ice crash over the back of his neck and all the way down his back. The hairs that clung to his skin rose to the sky in a standing ovation.

———————————

———————————

A crowd gathered at the cremation platform, prepared by the people of Katakonda for Edee. The structure stood in a clearing a short distance from the centre of the camp. Its four tall legs were secured with rope at the top to the supporting platform. The flatbed was wrapped with paperbark that cushioned his father's body.

Ted's skin was clean. His long curly hair flowed down his shoulders and rested on his back. A grey kangaroo skin wrapped his body and by his side was a woomera and spear from Katakonda for him to carry on his next journey. The shackled wounds on his ankles and wrists had been treated for the ceremony. He wore their marks as brandings of his final experiences. A painted sheet mask lay on his face; on it there were two dots for eyes, a triangle for a nose and a mess of painted curly hair.

Edee approached the platform with a lit fire stick. It was a long jarrah beam with a hair of fire on one end. He began the ceremony by resting the flame on the tinder that rested below. Leaving the lit torch, he went and stood by Kulanda.

"What happens now?" she asked.

"That's it. The rest is just a process."

"So where does he go?"

"Grandma says it's how our people get back to the spirit world. It's how we stay from wandering in the spirit. At the end, only his bones will remain, and that's the last of him. The last of him, like the last of yours, *MUST* be returned to my home country for the spirit to continue its journey."

The fire engulfed the platform and reached high into the night sky.

––––––––––––

The morning jolted Edee out of his rest and back into the crisis left by the attack. There was no real sleep in his grief. To wake was to leave a comfortable dream of days before and enter into a foreign reality.

His appetite had not joined him that morning, instead opting to sleep through despair. This did not stop him and he rose, charged with a sombre sense of purpose.

Edee went straight to work on the laragidi. The

woodiny had burrowed deep into the trees in this small forest. They'd devoured everything inside the living trunk from its base to its top. The tunnel they form is etched with smaller pathways for the white ants to travel, adding to the overall acoustics.

He knocked against logs testing for the most appropriate one. The wider the burrowed middle, the deeper the echo of his knock.

Their grey trunks extended beyond Edee's height. A thick one caught his attention. It was wide, about four hand lengths around. Edee knocked against it and was met with a deep thud. This one will do. He pushed against it and wriggled its weak roots. The soil that had grown the trees sprinkled into newly formed cracks and gaps.

Crunch went the wood.

Crunch crunch it sang again, until it finally lay uprooted on the ground. Edee shaved back the loose bark in preparation for marking.

He returned to the camp in search of a secluded area to be alone. Edee laid out the long pole in front of him and cut it to the length of his hips to the ground. After that, he ground down his ochre, mixing it onto his palette with a dab of goanna oil from days before. With a thin stick, he began to dab spots of paint over the burial pole.

Edee started with the first dot. *Us Yonga protect our*

children. He then let his instrument rest in the paint before spiralling it out clockwise from the centre. *We support our family and community.* The coil continued to grow, each new line encapsulating the next. *We overcome any fear with the direction of our ancestors.*

Edee continued the orbit around the central dot with a broken line all the way around. *Yonga, my people, give direction and are provided guidance by the spirit. Its balance and harmony guide us all.*

He saw the figure of a man sitting on the same flat rock he and Kulanda had been sitting on by the waterfall. He was too far away to distinguish any recognisable features. The man had a stack of fish and piles of wide-spanning damp paperbark. He took one fish and laid it in front of him, reached for salt crystals behind him and rubbed it over the fish.

In a stone mortar carved into a nearby boulder, Goolra ground leaves of lemon myrtle and peppercorn for his seasoning. When this was completed and rubbed on both sides, he'd wrap it in a thick leaf and place it with the rest.

Goolra looked up and caught Edee watching him prepare his catch of fish. The two shared a glance for a moment and exchanged a polite nod, as passers-by often do.

He moved to the fire and pulled the charred bones from their ashy cover. The ash stuck to the sweat in his palm and heaped into small clumps. They were rubbed off as he dusted the bones in preparation for their transportation.

Once they were clean and completely painted red, Edee placed them delicately into the hollowed log. There they would rest comfortably until their final return to the spirit world.

CHAPTER 12

The sun dawned on Edee's last day in Katakonda. A charred smell still hung on the air in the area. The country had been cleaned the best it could in such a short time. The children were returned to the camp that morning after the bodies had been addressed. Kulanda was talking with the young children by the river bank.

"Now, everyone. We need all of your help," she carefully addressed the staring kids. "There'll be plenty to learn in such a short time, but unfortunately this is required of you all now."

"What about my dad? Is he coming back?" asked a small girl.

"No, child. You will see them again one day, but no day soon."

The children sunk their heads towards the ground below in solemn acceptance.

"Edee! Wait up," Kulanda said. She turned back to the children, "Now! Nobody move. I've got a spotter amongst you. And they are going to tell me who was naughty while I was gone. They're secret though and will never reveal who they are, but they're watching!"

She hurried to catch up with Edee and Goolra further down the path. The children sat diligently in the eyes of the mythical spotter.

"You're leaving?" Kulanda asked.

"That's right, back to Karlaboodja," said Goolra before Edee could speak. Edee chuckled through his nose and awkwardly clutched his elbow with his hand.

Goolra continued, "Yeah, we'll head down through the forest below Badagurra. Shouldn't take us more than a few—"

"—Through the forest? But… we must follow the song lines," said Edee with an unsteady high pitch.

"Ah, stuff the song lines—my way is way quicker."

"I don't know…"

"Well. What should I do if they come back?!" asked Kulanda. "I can't handle everything all on my own!"

"You're not alone, Kulanda. There's help all around and we've doubled our scout patrols," replied Goolra, "and I won't be long at all. Not with my shortcuts, anyway." He shot a glance to Edee who was rummaging through his packed swag. "Besides they won't come back. What's left here for them anyway?"

Edee rummaged through his freshly packed swag

of things for something extra for Kulanda.

"Here! I have a message from Liara!" Edee jumped up from his crouch, momentarily lightheaded.

Kulanda looked over the stick carefully and traced the markings of her sister. Liara's voice spoke to her in that moment and a warm affection flowed over her.

Edee reached into his swag once again.

"These are some special nuts. They're a sedative. What I'm thinking is, wrap them in a pouch for next time they come… If they come. And you get up in the cave behind the waterfall and you put them in the water."

Goolra and Kulanda looked at each other.

"And then what?" asked Kulanda, confused.

"Well, when they can't find you—they might fill up on water from the stream. That'll make them really sleepy. Should be easy to handle then. If you get me." Edee wobbled at the knees and crossed his eyes, feigning intoxication. "Then just take the pouch out and let the stream run for a bit. It'll be all safe. So they tell me, anyways."

"Right, well, it's something, I guess. Thank you, Edee. Will you be coming back too?" replied Kulanda.

"Surely. I can't see why not," said Edee. Kulanda smiled and acknowledged with a gentle, happy grunt. "Well… bye then."

She turned so quickly it fanned her long hair into a glossy sheet.

"Come on," encouraged Goolra, "we have to get going to beat the sun."

———————

They had not made it past the borders of Katakonda before the sun fell below the horizon. The soft cotton clouds above set the fresh evening canvas. A deep red filled them from the setting sun that captured the entire sky.

"We'd better camp here," said Goolra.

"Sure thing."

The landscape was blanketed in a soft darkness of the setting sun. A pitch-black covering lay over everything below the red canvas sky. The final tips of the searing yellow sun still peeked from over the horizon in its last moments.

"Here, give me that. I'll take it up the hill," instructed Goolra, who proceeded to climb the loose gravel on the face of the incline.

The pole was heavy and uneven. Goolra felt its weight offset his left shoulder as he pushed uphill against the restless soil. Beads of sweat gathered on his forehead, searching for a coolness in the air.

In his hurry for respite, Goolra mis-stepped and slipped on the loose ground.

Edee turned to sounds of grunts, crashing and snapping twigs. He watched Goolra tumble in a heavy beat down the slope; the laragidi hit the ground with thuds behind him.

"Arghhh! My leg!" shouted Goolra into the approaching night.

The darkness had now consumed the sky and the burning yellows had faded to the other cheek of the world. Goolra lay on his back and stared at the canopy above, beneath the clouds.

"ARGHHH" exclaimed Goolra. He analysed how he came to be on his back, disappointed at his uncharacteristic loss of balance.

Edee rushed over to his side and dropped to his knees.

"Goolra! Are you alright?!"

"Yeah. My chest hurts and I think I've cut my leg."

Edee looked down at Goolra's right leg, which bore a deep gash, nearly to the bone. He quickly looked back at Goolra.

"Right… well… don't move. Don't look at your leg. Just. Don't move. I'll be back."

Edee rushed into the bushed area nearby to search for a remedy——and to fight back the nausea from seeing into Goolra's flesh. He squinted his vision in the darkness in hopes of increasing his sight but was limited to a short range of view.

You've got to look for the white fuzzy hair, with the red skull. That cocky apple fruit on the side, said his memory of his father treating his first cut from falling as a child. *Once you find it. You gotta grab that bark. Strip it all off like this here.*

The bark was laid out in front of Edee. He crushed it up into flakes and piled them into the bowl of his wunda.

Then you get some water. Just enough to cover the bottoms of the chips. Don't flood it now, or else you'll water it down too much. Mix it up like this.

Edee's actions matched the instructions of his father's memory.

That's a boy. You're alright. His father applied the antiseptic to a younger self in his memory. *Now, we need to find that tree orchid. White petals are what we're after. About the size of your thumb. We need that purple bulb in the middle there.*

Edee found the bush and picked about six flowers to take back to Goolra. The petals were soft against his coarse skin. He liked the way they played in his palm as he held them in a caged fist and let them rub against him.

"How's it going?" Edee asked Goolra when he arrived back.

"Yeah, just trying to relax, I guess," he replied in

good spirits.

Edee knelt beside Goolra's leg and applied the bark serum.

"Arghh! What about some warning? That stings!"

"Oh. Right. This is going to hurt too then."

Edee took the bulbs of the tree orchids and squeezed them into the disinfected wound. The sap oozed out of the pod and dripped into the cavernous flesh.

"ARGHHHHHH!"

"I told you," reminded Edee.

He emptied all the bulbs sap into the wound and pressed it closed with his attending hand.

"Can you hold this together?" asked Edee.

"Ah. Yeah, sure." Goolra grunted and groaned as he shuffled his body up and clutched his leg. The wound was much cleaner than it had been moments before and closed nicely.

Edee found an ant's nest nearby in the final light of the day. It was littered with small worker ants, bustling away with their tasks. He followed their line all the way to their nest. Around the small dirt mound were patrolling bull ants. They were at least six times the size of the worker ants and had two long pincers extending out from their face.

You have to grab them quickly. Around the body now. Don't let them turn back on you, instructed his father.

Edee pinched five of the bull ants and rushed back to Goolra.

"Almost done," Edee reassured, kneeling for a final time beside Goolra.

Edee took one of the ants and held it against the cut, with one pincer either side of the gash. The ant, pent up with rage, bit hard into Goolra's skin, driving his pincers deep. With a swift twist, Edee ripped off the ant's body, leaving the head firmly stapled to the wound.

"My grandfather used to tell me—Argh! Ouch!" winced Goolra while Edee attached the ant heads. "He used to tell me that we're living in our future memories. Ouch! And that you must take the good out of everything. It's all an opportunity to learn. Ouch! How do you wanna look back on it? he'd ask. As though you took the best or remembered the worst?"

Edee repeated the process another four more times until the ants were all gone and the wound was pinched shut.

The laragidi rested closeby, resilient and unshaken.

Edee left Goolra in search of firewood. His vision had adapted to the darkness so that he could make out shapes through the sea of the night. He found enough small pieces at the base of the trees and quickly returned to where Goolra was laying.

He laid his small shield on the ground. Edee got the kindling in a bundle in the bowl of the curve. He began to turn the stick quickly.

"Grandfather says that the fire has to be tickled out of the wood. And you can see the flame dance on top when it gets going," recalled Edee, excitedly.

Nothing happened. No smoke, no heat. Just a sore wrist. Goolra watched on and let Edee fail at a few more attempts.

"The wood's too damp, here," said Goolra and he shuffled around in his belongings.

He removed a brown lump of peat from his swag and carefully caressed it over towards the kindling. Goolra broke apart the thick marshy lump and blew into its centre, full of red-hot coals.

Smoke began to rise from the ignition in Edee's shield. Goolra continued to gently blow into the peat. With a poof, the flames jumped into the kindling. Goolra lightly sealed the lump and returned it to his swag.

"Wow! I've never seen something like that!" exclaimed Edee in surprise.

"A peat pouch?" Goolra asked. "No other way to get a fire started out here. You can't tickle damp wood, you know."

"How does it work? The peat?"

"It's an insulator. It holds the fire deep within.

Keeps it alive. Under all that darkness, squashed all together in there. Funny how it can stay burning, but it does. And when there's a break in the bog, well, plus a bit of breath, it can erupt into a blaze—as vibrant as before."

Edee transferred the fire to the pit on the ground. It jumped to the larger pieces of wood and crackled a warm glow over the area.

"Right then. That'll do for one day!" concluded Edee.

CHAPTER 13

The familiar smells of home greeted Edee as the pair neared the end of their journey. A fantastic cocktail of eucalypt and tea-tree settled in his nose. The weight of the laragidi dissolved in the swift relief of his return.

The pain in Goolra's leg had faded to a dull glow from its original fury. It had scabbed nicely into a deep red line of raised skin, crusted by sap and balm. His limp, although improved, had slowed them on their travels.

"Coo-ee," Edee lazily echoed the call into the breeze. His lips were cracked and etched with tiny red splits. He ran his tongue over them like a damp sponge over a stone. The soles of Edee's feet had hardened since last walking this path. The sands below, although unchanged, felt different to him.

Each step that Edee took closer towards Karlaboodja he felt further removed from his recent experiences. In the corner of his eye, he saw the figure of his youth playing between the trees. He turned to look at his past, but the memory was stripped away. The laragidi bumped against the bruises that littered Edee from bearing its long journey and disturbed his dreaming.

"Coo-ee." A strong wheeze rumbled with each breath Edee let escape.

Silence lay over the area as it had done for most of their journey. Then, from over a small ridge, a woman and two children popped their heads over the crest.

"Edee! Edee's back!" bubbled the voice with glee. The woman's tone was quickly interrupted at the sight of the laragidi and Edee's grim face.

"Oh, thank you… thank you…" she whispered to the winds, then looking at the two children next to her "Go! Jedda, Marlee. Go help him!"

The two ran out to Edee and Goolra as fast as they could.

"Let me take that," urged Jedda.

"Careful now. It's heavy" replied Edee.

"Here, lean on me," insisted Marlee to Goolra. The boy quickly moved under Goolra's arm and he supported his weight, helping him limp towards the central clearing.

"I'm alright," groaned Goolra in reaction.

"Now, now. Come on." Marlee was already carrying half his weight before he could protest a second time.

The four arrived at the central clearing. Jedda placed the laragidi delicately on the ground in the middle of the clearing. A wailing crescendoed over the community to usher the spirit on its cycle.

Goolra was taken away for further care by the healers and was left to rest.

Edee removed himself to a quiet area of the community in search of an unfamiliar peace. The cicadas ticked furiously in the warmth of the sun.

This is where he and Tilda would play in their life before. Their laughter echoed in Edee's memory as the visions danced before him. He imagined the footprints that once ripped through the soft earth around the community. Edee remembered the smells of the area that would rush his lungs as they both struggled to catch their breath through continuous laughter. He began to draw in the sand. First starting with her long flowing hair.

Tilda danced in the spooled tears that clung to the bottom of Edee's eyes.

A breeze, cooled by the shadows of the evening, played among the trees. It coiled itself around their trunks and hugged Edee below his skin. He shivered, wiped his tears and rubbed his palms against the sunburned outside of his arms.

On the ground, in the covering of bushes to Edee's side, was an unidentified rustling.

Probably just a lizard, Edee thought to himself. He closed his eyes and tried to imagine rest. He tried to abandon his recent hardship. Yet the more he tried, the louder those voices became.

The birds sang their melodies as they ushered in the night. They chirped to one another high above and rained their tunes on lucky ears below.

A rustling came from behind him again, this time closer and more empathic than before.

An eaglehawk hopped out of the bushes, flicking the leaves and sand into the air with its sharp talons. Bounce, bounce, bounce goes the bird. Kicking up a small dust cloud in its wake.

It had a plump body with grey and brown feathers. A small hooked beak perched below its bleeding black eyes. Its thick covering of feathers bounced too as the creature moved along with no clear objective. It hopped towards Edee with wings weakly outstretched, like it was holding up the hem of its long dress from the imaginary puddles below. The bird stopped beside Edee and stared at him with one eye.

Squawk! Squarrrarch, gruelll A soft growl settled deep within the bird's throat.

Edee furrowed an eyebrow and raised the other as he settled his heart from the startling alarm. He shuffled away from the bird and turned his back to the Eaglehawk.

The rustling continued behind Edee; he felt it building heavier in the ground. The tunes of delicate shuffling through leaves morphed to heavy, slow-paced and evenly spaced squashing and crackling. The light feathers turned to flesh and its bones grew into their new shapes.

"Now, now, boy. It isn't polite to ignore your elder," boomed a deep voice from behind him.

Edee sat up and snapped around to face the voice. Where there had first been an eaglehawk now was a grey-haired frail old man. He walked with back arched on itself as if he were a crescent moon drifting through the night sky.

"What the? Where'd you come from?!"

"You never really get used to it, you know," confessed the man. "Those feathers really irritate the skin. And my bones! The pain never gets any better."

The man was portly and wore a rounded salt and pepper beard. Short, straight matted hair topped his head. Once jet-black, it was now a soft grey on its way to white. He wore a large kangaroo pelt that was tied around his waist with a beautiful silken rope.

"Who are you?"

"Kadachi, Edee. I'm Karlaboodja Kadachi." He bowed, rubbing his arms. "Did I ever tell you about the time I got stuck as a wombat for years?"

"But, we've only just met…"

"Looong time to be out of form for. Waddling around the bush—it was actually pretty fun. Just the thought of getting stuck-stuck, you know. Like forever. That's not kinda fun."

Edee looked at Karlaboodja Kadachi. He could see how the wombat had stuck with his resemblance. Kadachi's face was wide and round like the moon. His eyes were comforting and brown; their gaze shot through Edee and stared into his shadow.

"Ooo yeah, I was a blubbery mess. Just couldn't get out of it. I'd wake up, mope around, back to sleep. I didn't bathe, eeurgh, I'm remembering the stink. Very strange time of life."

"Well, how'd you get back?"

"Consistent effort. Everyday. Consistently." Kadachi cleared his throat and continued. "Edee, we're going away for a while, you and I."

"To where? I've only just gotten back."

"There's a meeting of the clan. All the countries are coming together for a summit on climate, food resources, culture, religion, education, the lot. We'll discuss our issues, our quarrels and be with spirit.

Edee, disappointed he was not able to stay in his home and rest after such a long journey, did not react. Instead, he mentally withdrew and let the evening ride out. He needed rest and now that was the only thing he could think of.

"Oh, that reminds me. Did I ever tell you the story of the Seven Sisters? It started out that there was this boy, who liked a girl—as often the best stories start."

-END PART ONE-

CHAPTER 14

Ooooh, my head! Walken thought. I feel—I, I feeell slleepppyy.

The dam had hit her hard. She sloshed from side to side in a daze. Walken carved against the earth clumsily and bore great ditches out of the land and spiralled down to the earth.

As Walken spun, her rotations become narrower. The hole grew deeper, her spin became more centred and the rubble formed a tremendous bowl. It blocked the sun and cast a healthy shade over the clearing. In her confusion, Walken had bored the deepest she'd ever gone to rest. The wisps did the best they could in etching the finesse of the landscape.

Mmmmm. This will do, she thought as she wriggled into comfort and fell asleep.

"It's too quiet in here!" shouted Wooyan.

"Not with all your yabbering it isn't," replied Mirda.

"I need a river or some rustling—you hear that ringing? Like a high pitch 'teeeeeeeeeeeee…'?"

"ENOUGH!" yelled Nodjam and it shot through the side of the hole into silence.

"Moody…" teased Wooyan.

Kawa and Viola danced up the side of the carved earthen bowl.

"What if something fell down here?" asked Viola. "That'd be horrible."

They splashed a walkway here and climbing stairs there. Through the top edges, they punched holes to let more light through down to the bottom clearing where Walken was resting.

"LOOK OUT!" yelled Nodjam who shot through his tunnel and out the other side along the edge of the clearing. "COMING THROUGH!"

A rumbling followed him and its white noise crashed over the gorge. A violent stream of water chased Nodjam through as if the little wisp had stolen something, not even stopping to rest at the base of the bowl.

Viola and Kawa returned to the base to rest.

When the water eventually calmed, Nodjam returned to the rest of the wisps, puffing.

"There…," panted Nodjam searching for stamina, "will you be quiet now you have your river through?"

"Yes… yes I will," stammered Wooyan. "Thanks, Nodjam."

And they all slept.

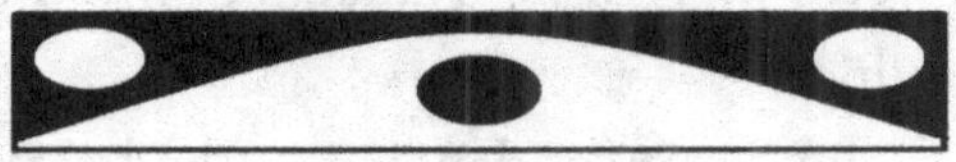

"Do you remember that time we were on the run through the bush from the swooping owl?" questioned Karlaboodja Kadachi.

"No, Kadachi. I don't think it was me you're remembering," Edee politely dismissed the old man.

Kadachi had not taken a moment to stop talking the entire journey to the meeting place. He'd recalled countless story after story from this time and the ones before. His newfound human form had restored his voice and he was making up for lost time.

"Yes, of course. Oh, that reminds me. Have I ever told you the story…" Kadachi paused on the spot and sniffed at the air. "Oh! We're here already?! Well, that was faster than I remembered. You're a great listener, you know!"

The colours of the landscape had faded around Edee. The hot light red of the desert sand simmered at his feet. He was tired from the travelling and was in desperate need of water. Everywhere he looked was undulating sand with a bleak welcome.

A stream babbled nearby in Edee's imagination.

"Do you hear that?" he asked emphatically, searching for its source.

"Oh yes. Ah, there it is." Kadachi pointed over Edee's shoulder.

There in the distance, dancing in the heat waves from the sand was a small pond bordered by a wall of lush green trees.

"Let's go!" Edee rushed over the hot sand, flicking it onto his back as he ran.

Kadachi lagged behind him and watched as Edee ran towards the oasis.

Edee drove his feet deep into the earth and propelled himself forwards, and the oasis took a step back. He pressed deeper, pushed harder and ran faster—but the oasis still retreated. Edee pushed and pushed, obsessed with quenching his thirst. At all costs he pushed deeper into the hot sand and ran harder, filling his lungs with a searing dust.

He bent further forwards and swung his arms violently, trying to increase his pace. The heat was broiling him from the inside. *If I just push it for a little bit longer. I'll make it and this will all be over,* he thought.

Edee came to a stop, panting over his dry throat and mouth. He propped his hands on his knees and bent over to dry reach. The sand around him faded from red, to black, and back to red as he struggled to maintain consciousness.

Kadachi approached with a few soft steps, his feet barely leaving a print.

"Come, Edee. You can't rush these things. Look at you—you've worn yourself out and we're not even a quarter of the way there," exclaimed Kadachi, picking Edee up and dusting off his skin. "Walk with me. Let us take one step at a time."

Edee was still catching his breath and Kadachi's words were muffled by the whirring flow of blood through his ears, like evening ocean waves. He rose to his feet, slumped over the frail man and began to put one foot in front of the other.

He watched carefully as the sand parted his toes. Their coarse symphony crashed over his raw skin. He thought about how long this sand had been undisturbed until marked by his tracks. He wondered who, if anyone, had walked this path before.

Edee gave attention to the detail of every step. He felt the sand become cooler as he walked more carefully through it.

"Ah, we're close," confirmed Kadachi, seemingly unfatigued from their travel.

Edee looked up from his steps to see the trunks of the bordering palm trees. The gentle waves of the pond, pushed by the breeze, lapped at the dry shore.

"Just through here." Kadachi led through the foliage of one of the low hanging trees.

Kadachi parted the greenery to reveal the secret landscape all around them. The newly parted gap opened a type of portal to an incredible paradise. A tremendous river ran through the middle of an alive shoreline, which fractured into a network of streams and creeks. Large cliffs surrounded the area, blackened by millennia of harsh suns. The masses of white water crashed over their surface and cooled them in the heat of the day.

Masses of birds flew in the sky. They moved as one solid mass, each following the prompts of the other, moving as one in harmony. Edee peered into the lush scene behind the curtain and then quickly back to his barren surroundings. He quickly switched his sights to the abundant scenery through the portal and then back to where he stood.

All of it was hidden in a dimension veiled in sacred protection.

"What… what is this place?" asked Edee, entranced by his first real taste of magic.

"Come on now," said Kadachi, leading with one foot through the portal.

Edee followed diligently and without question. Kadachi let the curtain fall when Edee was through and its opening vanished.

Kadachi dusted his hands.

"Well now. Where were we?"

A large herd of a thousand kangaroos bounded through bushland close by, the ground shook with their stampede. Their movement startled a sea of red-tailed black cockatoos that darkened the canopy above. Their shrieks rang between the trees and towards the large rock cliffs.

"There's no hunting here, Edee. Only in special times, you see." Kadachi picked the largest rose plum Edee had ever seen and began peeling it. "You can take what you like during this time. Just don't take more than you need. Ok? It's that simple. Otherwise, there'll be less next time."

Edee followed Kadachi closely; his uncertainty about this new place grew a great discomfort within him.

Edee stood at the mouth of the giant bowl carved in the earth. A continuous path spiralled around its inner face down to a large circular clearing at the base. As Edee walked down the path, the paintings on the wall to his left jumped from their rocky canvas and played in his imagination as Edee walked down the path.

He was close to the bottom of the inverse dome. Groups of people had begun to arrive informally and were gathered in various groups around the clearing.

"YES, YOU DID! I SAW YOU!!!" yelled a voice from within the huddled circle.

"Did what?! You didn't see nothin'," replied another.

"Don't lie to me! When we crossed, at the border. You knew that kill was mine."

"I didn't know nothin'."

"You're right there!"

"Hey, I killed it fairly. My arm, my kill."

"Your arm your kill," mocked the accuser. "Anyway. I wanna settle it. I'd practically done it in with my boomerang and you come in and finish him with your waddy and took it home with you! That ain't right."

"Wait, seriously? There's, there's really no need for that," replied Monaro nervously.

"NUP!" Yarren declared defiantly. "I'm sick of it! Front up."

If there is a quell of unresolved conflict, it must be concluded before the proceedings can begin. In this open landscape, cluttered with an influx of arriving dignitaries, two parties faced off, barking furiously without restraint, as men do. They gathered to let the spirits decided if the accused is to be guilty or innocent.

Their harmony of shouting was incoherent, the hostile tone was communicating the atmosphere clearly. There was an apparent language barrier and the solution of arguing louder did not seem to be bridging this.

"Do you think he did it?" asked Waru to Yarren.

"No. I mean, he did. But I don't really care. Truth is, I got a bigger one later that day anyway. I just want to shake him a little. Have some fun," replied Yarren.

They both chuckled as Yarren began to surrender his belongings, except his spear.

Monaro had done the same. He now stood facing Yarren, his knees knocking with tremors.

Yarren and Monaro now faced one another at a distance that shrunk them in their vision. Yarren traced a launch line in the sand with the heel of his foot.

"You better not go over that line!" yelled Monaro.

"Yu betta not go over mleh mlehh," whispered Yarren mockingly under his breath.

Yarren slowly walked away from the line, counting his paces. He swivelled on his feet at step ten and turned to face his target. Yarren brought the spear to his ear, his arm poised and ready to launch. With rapid side steps, Yarren leaned back and launched the spear with full force.

I'll just scare him, he thought with a cheeky grin.

The spear hissed through the air. Monaro stood as strong as he could as it hurled toward him.

THoonk The spear missed and buried itself in the loose sand beside Monaro.

"HA! Told you!!! You can't aim anyway!" Both parties erupted in laughter. "You couldn't hit water down by the river!! HAHAHA," yelled Monaro, clutching at his sides.

"What?! I missed on purpose! You little! Get me another spear!!" Yarren lunged for a second spear at his side but was stopped by Waru, red in the face with laughter.

Edee walked away from the gathering, his hands gently crossed behind his back. They bumped against him with each step as he casually wandered the central clearing.

There was cheering coming from the other side and he went over for a closer look. A build-up of cheering was followed by a *thud*, a moment of pause and more cheering soon after. Edee's stride crackled the dried brown leaves beneath him as he walked with a leisurely pace.

The trees opened to a vast expanse of grass. Its thick green blades were cool under Edee's feet, as if he were walking over a carpet of crisp feathers over-laid on one another. A pack of spotted boys and a few men who refused to surrender their youth gathered in a group at one end of the makeshift arena. They were politely roughhousing; small shoulder bumps and even a few cheeky jabs in the ribs were the idle activities of the group.

Still in the clearing, but far from the group, stands one boy holding a clump of woven Typha roots of the bulrush stuffed with leaves and vines. Almost shaking with anticipation, the boy winds back his right leg, drops the clumped ball and punts it wildly towards the group.

The small gathering, as if choreographed, took a slight crouch in their knees while the ball hurled towards them. They all jumped. The better athletes rose to the top of the group. Four pairs of hands were in contention for possession, but anything could happen. A short competition ensued and a small triumphant boy made the leaping catch, riding on the backs of his bigger cousins and brothers.

He jogged through the pack and past the boy who kicked it into the group, switching spots to take his position as the kicker.

CHAPTER 15

Edee and Karlaboodja Kadachi stood at the edge of the enormous hole carved into the earth and watched the opening ceremony. All around its internal walls was a clockwise spiral walkway that bore deeper in the ground. The wide-open mouth spiralled to a narrow gullet with a flat clearing at the base of its throat. The clearing was spotless, not a grain of sand out of place. Everything had to be just right.

In the centre of the base was a series of wooden poles affixed in the ground and formed in a circle, slanted in towards the centre. Beneath them, laid out in the centre of the formation, was a large bundle of dry bark and thin twigs.

Off to the side ran a gentle stream leading in from the rivers nearby. The tunnel that bore into the base of the throat was smoothly carved within the ground and the water gushed as it flowed through.

"It's going to be some sunset, Edee," observed Karlaboodja Kadachi, looking at the thin cloud cover that had splattered the awaiting canvas.

"Do you remember the last one, Karlaboodja?" said a voice from behind them.

They both turned to see Bilyakep and Katakonda Kadachi.

"Oh, yes, quite well," replied Karlaboodja Kadachi. "Good to see you both. This is Edee. He'll be joining us today."

The new arrivals looked Edee up and down.

"Is this the one then?" asked Bilyakep Kadachi.

"He's a bit scrawny, don't you think?" added Katakonda Kadachi. With a soft smile, he huffed a gentle laugh out of his nose.

"I'm pretty sure. We'll see either way," replied Karlaboodja Kadachi.

Edee stood there and watched the conversation with a concerned silence. No one had looked to him for input, yet he was all they talked about. He bounced his head around the discussion in search of familiar context that might include him in the subject.

"Oo, look. The ceremony is beginning," interjected Bilyakep Kadachi.

A small orchestra had gathered at the bottom clearing of the large bowl. They began their melody with the boorns leading the beat. The didgeridoos followed close behind and joined to dance up through the acoustics of the spiral throat. The music leapt to the sky and danced back down the trail of the carved path.

Seven women, all painted from head to toe in white ochre, came into vision at the top of the canyon. Their dance was fluid and moved swiftly with grace. Tied to their biceps and thighs were strands of multi-coloured baubles. They moved their arms around their heads, shook their hips and shuffled their legs. The baubles danced all around them. They played chasey around the women, weaving in and out, colliding and fleeing from each other. Each of the women carried a small piece of wood, which they placed on the kindling in the centre of the poles before taking their place around the fire pit. Then a stream of country delegates began to flow down the spiral pathway. Their colours moved uniquely from the rest, which unified them all the same.

Edee saw a man and woman dressed entirely in shells. Their heads bore parrot feathers tied on a string of woven shore reeds. They each wore a chest piece of beaded shells on the same woven lace. The patterns were a captivating mix of small cream stones, large green shells and random trinkets of accent.

They moved with a steady step but alternated between a crouch and stand in a smooth rhythm as if sifting through a gentle ocean.

"Kadachi?" Edee asked.

"Yes?"

"Yes?"

"Yes?" said all three.

"Who're they?" Edee elaborated, pointing at the beautiful shell designs.

"Djaluma Island. Whale totem," said Katakonda Kadachi dismissively.

"Whale totem. Wow." Edee exhaled and returned his gaze to the stream of nations.

He saw the wallaby marking of Badagurra. Their dress was a combination of kangaroo furs and duck feathers for highlights. They performed their dance lazily as they moved with the group. Edee squinted into the crowd and recognised one face, although sickly and thin since he last saw it clearly. The rest of their group were very young and seemed lost in the new world. They moved confused, trying to keep up with what to do. Badagurra placed their pieces of wood on the pile that was building at a steady pace.

The orchestra had now taken on three more musicians from newly arrived countries. Their instruments added to the piece and drove the wave higher into the sky. It bounced from wall to wall and danced out of the mouth like a megaphone.

Bilyakep entered from the stream bored through the earth. Their bodies were painted with white ochre to trace the pathways of their internal life force. They each wore a red lower covering and a red headband lined with feathers. Poking out the back of their long, thin, two-person canoes were three-pronged spears. For the ceremony, they each bore a different tassel, soaked in ochre for highlights. A black strand clung to the left spike, a bright yellow to the middle and a deep red on the right.

The wood stack in the middle of the clearing had grown to a significant height with the contributions of each community. An orchestra of fifteen musicians now belted their melodies into the sky. The vibrations on the surface of the earth gently rumbled the soles of Edee's feet. The penultimate delegates made the journey down the spiral pathway, added their wood pieces, and took their place.

The music came to a sudden and synchronised stop with the loud clap of a pair of musical boorns. Silence blanketed the area.

A single group stood at the top of the bowl on the beginning of the path. Each man was covered in rich red dust from his home soil. They all had a torch that blazed violently against the first shadows of the early night. An acapella chant broke out from the red country group. One of the members rolled their tongue with a high-pitched howl to the evening sky. This prompted the group to begin their journey to the base.

Their legs were painted with wavy lines of white ochre, which combined into one at their pelvis and continued up their chest towards a white circle around their solar plexus.

They danced and shook their legs quickly from side to side. Their markings moved wildly over their bodies behind the light dust screen in the air. An illusion of a legless troop wobbled their flames down to the slope and towards the awaiting clan.

"Kadachi?" asked Edee.

"Pilup country. Home of the original mountain. They bring with them the original fire, still burning today, passed on from Walken," answered Karlaboodja Kadachi, expecting the question.

Each of the Pilup members had orbited a full rotation with their flames around the gathered countries at the base of the bowl. They took their individual positions surrounding the wood pile. All together, they raised their torches into the air and slowly lowered them onto the kindling below.

The fire *woofed* as the ignition burst into the awaiting wood. At that point, the orchestra, without a missed beat, jumped back into their harmonised piece. This time the music erupted with the fire and breathed a life into the flames from all around. They licked at the night sky as a warmth filled the canyon.

The ends of the poles that formed a circle around the clearing had caught fire and burned strongly. A representative from each community stood and removed a pole from the fire and placed it at the back of their position around the circle.

"Ahhh, I love that ceremony. Now that's over. It's your turn, Edee," said Karlaboodja Kadachi.

"My… my turn for what?" replied Edee.

"For the real ceremony!" interjected Bilyakep Kadachi, excitedly. "Oh, I remember mine. You're going to hate it! Ha! Come on now. This way."

CHAPTER 16

Walken was sailing through the dreaming, inspecting the earth below. The canopy blurred passed like a colour wheel, all shades of green and yellow playing amongst each other. A pillar of smoke towered on the horizon and puffed black clouds into the sky. She hurried to the smoke to investigate. The green in the trees began to fade to an autumn brown. The leaves were plucked from their grasp in the edification left from Walken's haste. They fell softly to the ground and crumpled to dust under the weight of their own frailty.

As she got closer to the smoke, the life below continued to fade. The trees now bore no leaves and stood like gravestones on infertile ashen soil. The branches were gnawn down to the stump, wood chips wildly flung as shrapnel of the murderous carnage.

The black smoke bellowed into the air. It burned behind a fence that Walken could not see through. Surrounding the community was a clearing of stumps worn down to the root that stretched further than Walken could see. They had been torn apart on impulse. Without regard and without restraint. Way out there, in the middle of nowhere, was this camp.

Walken was close enough to see through the wire fence that surrounded the community. There were corrugated tin shacks littered all around the camp. They were single room low built houses with rusted holes speckled all over. There were people scattered throughout. Their heads hung low, covering their faces in a blinding shadow.

She touched against the fence to get a closer look.

ZZAAAAPPP!

The fence shocked her and jolted her back.

"OUCH! DAMN!! OUCH OUCH, DAMN!!!!" she exclaimed.

No one from within the camp flinched at the sound. They continued about in their zombie state, swaying aimlessly. Their bones stretched in their skin with malnourishment. Thin veils of wispy hair fell into their faces.

One small child looked up from where she was sitting with her legs crossed. She looked directly at Walken.

"Child! What is this place? What has happened to you?!" Walken pleaded, panicking and tearing at the impenetrable barrier.

The little girl's face was still directed at Walken, her features suffocated by shadow.

"Child! Are you ok?!"

The girl's eyes flashed open with a fiery red. Her mouth drooped open and a slimy strand of saliva flooded over her lip. Her gaze remained fixed on Walken. The little girl's lips struggled furiously to scream out.

help me   help me

Walken saw her muffled cries and whipped into a frenzy. She circled the entire camp for any way in.

ZAP* *ZZAP* *ZAAAPP

The fence bit at her as she threw herself against it.

She flew high into the sky, searching for any possible way in. The smell from above was of seared hair and charred devastation. There, in the centre of the clearing, was a grand statue. It stood in bronze glory, a fat brooding figure with pushed in snout, greasy slicked back hair and an ill-fitting red jacket. A thick tome in one hand and a rifle in the other.

Walken and her wisps flew east in a rage towards smoke on the horizon.

Away from the dreaming, Edee was walking with other Kadachi through the woods. The group of Kadachi hummed a gentle tune. One would lead a melody and another would reply. The conversation jumped around the group and danced around Edee.

"What, what song is that?" asked Edee

"Hmm? Oh, were we singing?" queried Bilyakep.

"We're humming again, aren't we?!" asked Katakonda, "I thought we all agreed. No. more. Humming. It tickles my throat." *cough, cough*

"You're the one that started it!" piped in Bada-gurra.

"So, it isn't a spirit song? A map for our journey?" asked Edee.

"A map? The number of times I've walked here, it's like a memory. It's just a tune boy. Relax. We're nearly there," replied Karlaboodja.

The drone of a single didgeridoo rolled in from the distance. It rumbled in the earth and bounced into Edee's toes. The leaves applauded its arrival with a gentle rustle in the breeze.

Edee was struck by the first sight of the cave. He stalled his step for a moment to gawk at the entrance. The mouth of the open cave gargled out the drone of the didge. The throat was lined with quartz crystal all the way down into its depths.

A magnificent light shone through the dark night. The deeper down through the earth, the brighter it shone. The base of the didge fluttered in Edee's chest and rattled his rib cage.

"Now," insisted Karlaboodja, "this is definitely going to hurt. But remember, if you die—you won't feel it anymore… so there's that. And if you live, we'll fix you up in no time. So, it's only temporary. It's always only ever temporary."

"And," Bilyakep added, "you're going to see some things."

"Durrr," uttered Badagurra.

"Can you not interrupt me?! I'm still refining my script. We don't do this very often you know?!…" Bilyakep cleared his throat. "You might—you will— become an animal. But again, like with anything, you'll figure it out eventually if you just hang in there. Heh, at my initiation, I vomited."

"And lastly," chimed in Katakonda, "you have to come back. You must return through the water to complete the transition. Otherwise, well." He looked at the first, "Death, was it?"

"Probably. I don't imagine it's good though, to get stuck over there," replied Karlaboodja. "Oh, and don't look at them in the eyes."

"Don't look at who in the eyes?" asked Edee with a

confused inflection.

"The Wul…"

A second didgeridoo interrupted the Kadachi and joined the first. No more words were said. Their pitches married well and tickled Edee's lungs. Loose rocks danced across the ground as it shook with increased force.

The etched quartz walls shone brighter. Edee's knees became weaker as his vision blurred.

"I don't feel well. I better sit dow—" Edee fell to the ground in an unconscious lump.

"There we go," exclaimed Karlaboodja. "Right, you two pick him up. Let's go for a wander down to the water."

The small party entered the cave, carrying our unconscious friend.

He was standing beside the gathering as a shadow of himself. Edee's shadow watched them carry his body away, yet he remained standing in the opening of the cave. His skin hummed as if overcharged with static.

The depths of the once vacant cave now opened to a secret paradise of lush green grass, abundantly fruitful trees and water so clear it seemed invisible. Its surface was so crisp and pure you would rather thirst than disrupt its perfection with a sip.

The illusion of a stream of flowing glass led on well beyond the horizon. Animals pranced along its banks and birds danced against the sky.

"Kaya, Shadow," said Kenny. A tall, slender figure wrapped in a huge fur stood before Edee. It was at least twice as tall as Edee and as skinny as yearling branches on a budding white gum.

The figure's face was covered with a shadow mask. Its darkness was pitch black and completely covered all its features. Two bright blue lights shone from its eyes as it peered back into Edee's shadow.

"Kaya," Edee replied, distracted. He watched the Kadachi carry him away into the cave that now shone with the light from the quartz-lined walls. His limp arms dangled as if dead. He looked into his eyes and saw nothing. Just meat. All of him was standing where he was in this moment.

"Let's talk a small walk," suggested Kojak and draped his long gangly arm around Edee's shoulder.

They took one step and the earth moved like a tread-mill. The Wulgi remained stationary and brought their reality forward to meet them. In one stride, they could cover hundreds of kilometres—all at the pace of a leisurely stroll. They took another step and were beyond the horizon, Edee had seen at the opening of the cave.

He looked back to see the mouth of the cave, but its portal had vanished into a lush field of green.

This must be the nausea they told me about. The world whooshed around him.

In the physical world below, beside and in between, the Kadachi were tending to Edee's lifeless body. They laid him gently on the rock bed and placed his head on a pillow of gathered foliage. The stone had been worn over thousands of years to form the necessary place markers for the ceremony. Each footstep from generations before still remained in the cave; their footprint secured in the earth for all to see.

Bilyakep placed feathers of the eaglehawk over Edee's arms, chest and legs. His body remained motionless.

A third didgeridoo joined the harmony. Their combined drone pierced into both worlds. They were calling for help.

The four Wulgi stood around Edee. Red dirt clung to their feet—the greenery of the lush forest is a long time away now. A giant mountain brooded over the group. A deep drone pierced the spiritual realm and resonated in the chest of Edee's shadow.

"Welcome Edee, to this place. The beginning," soothed Koko.

"See everything around you. The movements and shapes that play against each other. Do you see it all? Look how they dance in perfect harmony, Edee," directed Kojak.

"Look at the way they all care for one another. They use their strengths to help other's weaknesses. They unite and work together," observed Kenny.

"Now, look closely for him, he will be your target - the whole reason we brought you here," urged Koko, "because we're still not sure how he got here."

"For who?" questioned Edee.

"The, Fart!" replied Dom with a sherlockian intensity.

"The what?"

"Shh, you!"

The Kadachi knelt beside Edee's body. They each removed large brown feathers from their pouches and placed them gently on Edee. They covered his arms and legs, each standing when they were done.

Edee's shadow turned his back to the Wulgi and inspected the expanse of the area. There were healthy flowing falls, impossibly strong streams of water and lush ever-growing forest, all with the echoes of hundreds of animal species.

When he turned back, there were four Wulgi as eaglehawks perched and looking back at him.

"Well," squawked one of the eagle hawks, "we should go now."

Edee's shadow's skin became itchy. His flesh squirmed all over and he felt it wriggle away from his bones. He convulsed and scratched at the bumps.

A single feather sprouted from his forearm.

"Argh!!" Edee squealed and shook his entire arm.

Another four feathers appeared as he shook. His legs itched too and feathers of the eaglehawk sprouted there as well.

He fell to the ground in a hunch. The face of Edee's shadow morphed into a beak and the beady eyes of the bird.

"Now that you're ready. We'll head out," instructed Kenhawk, Kenny as eaglehawk.

In sequence, they each spread their wings and sprang into the air with a sturdy gust.

Edee watched from his new height in amazement, before spreading his wings, giving a solid thrust and landing firmly on his chest.

"**Oompf!**" he exclaimed.

"**Come on, Edee. You're thinking like a human. And humans can't fly, silly,**" sniggered Domhawk.

Edee steadied himself and gave it another try. He leapt into the air and maintained his flight with the group.

I'M FLYING!!! LOOK AT THIS!!! HAHAAA! he screamed in his thoughts.

The Kadachi tended to Edee's unconscious body and lit a fire for warmth. A cloud of thick smoke billowed from the flames as they added a covering of thick green eucalyptus leaves. It smelled like winter. A thick plume filled the cavern and penetrated the two worlds. A deep fire burned within.

The five eaglehawks flew with immense speed. The land below whooshed in a blur. A thick smoke crept in from the horizon. It lingered there and the earth slowed beneath them. Slowly the smoke began to consume the sky with its black clouds. All that was faded around it as the thick grey smog reached further and further.

In single file, they flew directly for its heart. Edee

the eaglehawk was the last in line.

Kenhawk tucked its wings and dived straight for the flaming centre of smoke. Its feathers singed and coiled in the flame. Its beak melted as it scratched the impervious surface. Then, in a flash, it was vaporised into nothing.

Kohawk, directly behind, tucked its wings and continued the dive. It saw the devastation of the previous bird but maintained its course steadfastly. Its feathers steamed and its claws dripped. And, in a flash, it was consumed by flame.

Domhawk followed suit, determined to persist towards thir goal. It broke through deeper into the barrier and dived closer to the increasing temperatures. Again, the bird met the same fate and was puffed out of existence.

Kokohawk pushed harder and faster. He could feel the flesh and feathers stripping from his body. Edee was close on his tail.

The flames raged with immense heat and Kokohawk combusted into ash. Edee the eaglehawk felt as if he'd been diving for an age. He couldn't breath or feel anything other than the consistent burning of the fire that licked at his skin. His feathers melted away from him and exposed his flesh. A flash of blinding white light filled his vision. And then? Nothing.

Edee's shadow landed on the ground and felt the coarse sand on the arches of his feet. He had returned to his original form.

There was no place for magic here, beyond the fire. The earth was a fine dust, void of substance. Edee's shadow walked through the camp. Rusted corrugated tin shacks propped each other up in one lumpy mess. Each hovel served as an oven that cooked its residents in the relentless heat of the sun.

A body shuffled past Edee's shadow.

"Hey, you. Where am I?" he asked.

The person slowly turned to look at the shadow——her eyes hollow pits of pitch black and mouth slack-jawed.

There was no response, just a vacant look. And she continued to roam the camp with the area's characteristic lifeless shuffle.

"You see, all these people are lost," said Kenny into Edee's mind.

"We can't quite figure out how this happened, this place," added Koko telepathically.

A large statue of Bunyip stood tall and proud in the centre of the camp. His chest staunchly posed to the sky. A thick book of rules in one hand and a rifle to enforce them in the other.

"There he is!!!" exclaimed Dom.

More bodies poured into the camp from the sky above, six or seven at a time like a rain of death. As each one hit the ground, the statue grew larger. The people picked themselves off the ground and began their eternal wander.

They toiled for Bunyip without the ability to renew. Their shadows were trapped. Each one a hollow being responding to captivity. The landscape bubbled and morphed around them. The brooding statue grew, expanding in all directions.

"No! We can't leave yet! WE HAVE TO DO SOMETHING!" screamed Edee to the Wulgi watching outside the camp.

The earth morphed through the flames, back through the smoke, over the forests and red dust, and arrived back to the quartz-lined cave.

The Wulgi removed their upper clothing and let them fall to the ground. Stretched over the chests of each Wulgi, about the size of an outstretched hand, were glowing markings. They were all bordered by a circle. Each marking was unique to the Wulgi and they glowed a pulse that matched the beat of the drone.

They threw their shoulders back and let a blinding beam of light escape from their markings. The light was absorbed by Edee's shadow. His eyes shone bright like two spotlights into the clouds.

Karlaboodja Kadachi removed a large circular stone

from the white-hot ashes of the fire. An extensive pattern had been carved delicately on its face. It sizzled as he clutched it with dampened paperbark. He calmly walked over to Edee's unconscious body and placed the stone on his chest.

Edee's skin seared and smoked under the stone.

You never get used to the smell, thought Karla-boodja Kadachi to himself.

Bilyakep and Badagurra Kadachi's made small incisions in Edee's skin with razor-sharp stones. They gently drew the blade over his index finger and peeled back a portion of skin. Underneath, they placed a shard of quartz and sealed the wound. These small cuts were made all along his arms and legs, each one planted with a tiny quartz seed.

The landscape morphed around Edee's shadow and the Wulgi once more. They arrived at a small pool of water. It was not wide enough to be called a pond, but was bigger than a puddle. It looked shallow and refracted a crystallised spectrum of light in the water.

"Edee will not have survived this experience. The trauma would be too much, both physical and mental. Shadow, you will now be called Andee," announced Koko.

The Kadachi lifted and moved Edee's corpse to the shores of the nearby stream. They gently laid him down and splashed water on his chest wound.

"Remember to look out for the fart! He'll be tricky. Probably in disguise. But you'll smell him, sure enough," instructed Dom.

"Go now, Andee. You have much to do," encouraged Kojak.

Andee's shadow dived into the multicoloured pool sinking to stand on the bottom, as he thought to himself, Humans can't breathe underwater so don't think that way.

The Kadachi submerged the head of the corpse into the stream. The body began convulsing and struggled for air.

He was lifted out of the water and Andee was born. His body was weak and battered, his soul bruised and vulnerable. A firm breeze rattled the leaves on the trees above and whisked Andee off into a deep sleep.

"Tilda…!" he whispered out an exhausted and delusional cry. "Oh Tilda, I had a terrible dream."

CHAPTER 17

Andee had been walking for some seasons since the clan meeting. His journey began slowly, still recovering from the turmoil of his transition. But as time went on, he healed and became stronger.

His strides were long at his new height of over six feet. His lean calf muscles capture his weight with every step as they rippled under his skin. Tree trunk like quads guided his steps toward his destination. His skin was now covered in small raised scars from the ritual, almost like the scales of a crocodile. The deep black pupils bordered by the soft browns in his eyes were illuminated by their new glow. Like a soft night-light, his eyes pulsated a gentle radiance.

He wore a large grey kangaroo pelt that had been masterfully treated to be the softest Andee had ever worn. The wound underneath his garments had healed well and now bore the intricate markings of the carved stone. His new pants scraped on the ground as he walked, but he paid them no mind. He was only focused on the path ahead.

On the tree to his right was a sign for a waterhole coming up on the left. Andee pitched a coo-ee into the distance. He did not stop with the same formality as he had done in the past and simply tossed the words into the air without serious consideration.

"COO-EE!" echoed back from the distance. Despite his casual yell, Andee's heart rate still spiked with an influx of nervousness.

A slender man peeked his head over the crest of the embankment on the left side of the trail. He squinted his eyes down the path towards Andee and shaded his brow with an outstretched hand.

"Edee?! Is that? IT IS!! HEY EDEE'S HERE!!" yelled the man down the bank to the shores. He ran over to where Andee was walking up the path.

"Edee!" continued Kalanga, "how about that?! What're you doing all the way out here? Woah! Look at your eyes! What's happened? HA! That's great. I love 'em!"

Andee, trying to get a word in, repeatedly went to respond but was immediately cut off.

"Come, come. You have to see the others," insisted Kalanga.

He hurried down the loose soil of the hill to the banks of the river. Andee clutched his things tight to his torso and slowly descended the slope. The soil swallowed his feet, but his balance remained unphased, and he made it to the bottom unhurt.

"Hey, look! It's Edee from Karlaboodja!" introduced Kalanga.

"Edee!" chorused two voices in unison.

"Actually, I'm Andee now. I'm not Edee anymore, not quite. I remember what if felt like, to be him, but I'm too different now," explained Andee.

"Oh! That must have been exciting. Tell us everything!" begged Kolunga.

"Yeah! We don't often get to hear these stories. Grandfather won't let us beyond the song lines," encouraged Jilungo.

Others gathered around Andee in anticipation of the tale of his journey. What he'd seen, done, heard and felt along the way. They implored him to share his experiences and relished the opportunity to live vicariously through the traveller. They all gathered, the original six from their first meeting, plus three more, to greet Andee. All except one woman. Andee noticed her through the crowd and she immediately stole his attention.

She sat by the creek with her left arm bound in a rudimentary sling. Its weight hung heavy on her neck and dragged her posture down to her knees. Andee went deaf to the crowd and their requests for entertainment. He gently pushed through the gathering and proceeded over to the solemn girl on the shore.

"Are you all right?" he teased her, hoping for a smile.

"Hmm?" she looked up from her trance.

"Your arm. You must be all right?" he repeated, immediately realising she had heard him.

"Oh, funny stuff," she replied with an adolescent dismissal.

Kalanga and Kolunga followed Andee over to the girl.

"Poor child. She was climbing trees last season and slipped from the top. Fell all the way down and hit every branch too. I saw it," recalled Kalanga.

"I told her not to, but up she went anyway!" added Kolunga.

Andee looked back to the girl and knelt beside her. He took her arm in his hands.

"ARGHHH!" she screamed, a tear leapt from her eye and trickled down her cheek.

There was a wound up her bicep that was littered with shards of bark and plant material. It had festered and was surrounded by a soft yellowy-white goop. The ball of her shoulder was lodged out the front of her socket, her arm bulged forward and hung down lifelessly.

"Oh my. You've done quite a good job here," observed Andee.

He retook her arm in both hands and began to

hum a tune. As he hummed its drone, he began to manipulate the joint in a figure eight motion. She winced with every movement and recoiled away from Andee.

"There there, the pain won't last much longer," he reassured her. "Just relax as best you can."

Without warning and with full force, Andee yanked on the girl's arm, relocating it into its socket. A large chunky crack rang through the ears of those nearby.

"I… I have to go," stammered Kalanga who fled quickly holding his stomach.

Kolunga stood still and looked on, his eyes wide open and his flesh pale.

A warm crash flooded over the girl's entire body which flushed away the pain of her internal injury. Andee could now move the joint with far more ease and without discomfort to the girl. He continued the figure eight motion to assist the liquids to settle the joint.

Andee moved his attention to the open wound sustained during the fall. He assessed she was most likely impaled by a branch as she descended.

He took a thick piece of bark from a nearby tree and cleansed it of its loose sediment. Andee placed the edge of the bark shard on the infected wound. With a slow firm movement, he scraped to free the infected scab and to reveal a fresh pink wound. He discarded the bark and brushed around the wound with his fingers.

"Now, I am sorry for this next part," Andee apologised to the young girl.

Andee's index finger began to glow furiously. It let out a blinding light that broke Kolunga from his trance and forced him to cover his eyes.

Andee drove the shining finger into the wound. The skin seared and smoked.

"ARGHHHH!!!" she screamed in agony.

Andee slowly removed his finger from the wound. As he pulled away, the skin healed behind it. The fibres of her flesh joined together after being touched by Andee's light and stitched themselves anew.

The wound was sealed and Andee ran his finger over the surface of her skin, clearing any sign of the original injury.

"There. I know it was painful, but you're all better now! Thanks for being so strong," reassured Andee.

The girl wiped away tears from her eyes. Her shoulder was still stiff and tender when she tried to move it but was clearly better.

"Thank you, thank you, thank you!" she sobbed, through tears of relief.

During this time, the abandoned crowd had slowly migrated over to the pair by the creek.

"Whoaaahhh," gawked Kolunga. "So, it looks like you've got a few stories to share, Andee. Go on, then! I'll get a fire started. We'll stop here tonight. Tell. Us. Everything."

Andee camped with the wanderers and exchanged stories of their adventures.

CHAPTER 18

The wind moved over Walken with a furious haste. Her hearing whooshed as her heart pumped a thick, toxic sludge through her.

What have you done you…?!! She began preparing her berating in her head, but the words struggled to find their place at the rate of her heart.

Gahh!! Walken let a tornado escape from her in a boiling frustration.

In the distance, she saw some thick lumpy grey blocks. They were spewing smoke into the air, but this was not smoke from wood or leaves. Its columns were an impenetrable black soot. It looked like a ruptured bowser puffing into the sky.

The clearing of the trees stretched wide like a cancerous mole. Stumps rose from the ground and stood to attention like diligent tombstones in a graveyard. All around them were splintered trunks, reduced to tinder in the destruction, their remains stained with halitosis. The horizon was consumed by the clearing.

There was no song in the area—it had been wiped clean. The earth watched on silently at Walken's return. There was no chirping, babbling, howling or rumbling; just a dying silence.

The wisps played among the rubble of the forest. First, they sang soft melodies to the damaged earth. They tried all the songs they knew, in every key they could, but the rubble did not budge. It stared back at them between the gaps of the lifeless shrapnel of the once lush forest.

Then they tried dancing with the land.

Surely that would work, they thought to themselves. They danced as hard as they could. They pulled off every movement flawlessly and even broke out some freestyle moves for good measure.

"Hmm. Nothing," dismissed Mirda.

"I don't get it, that's all we did before," pondered Wooyan.

"Is someone not meaning it enough?" asked Mirda, looking around at his companions.

"Meaning it?" asked Kawa.

"I really think that you have to be in the dance, you can't just bop along," explained Mirda.

"I don't really mean it," yawned Nodjam from the back. "I'm just so tired. I'm fading, guys. Just going to… wander… off over… here," and Nodjam fell asleep.

"Oh! I know!" excitedly yelled Yoont from the back, "we can play chasey again! That'll work!"

The wisps played under Walken as she continued to investigate the obliteration of the once thriving and diverse forest.

But nothing would grow.

"Eeurgh," she huffed and shot into the air in a flash to continue her search.

"WHERE IS HE?!" Walken yelled in a rage.

She propelled herself with a sonic boom towards the grey blocks in the distance. A horrid smell of vinegar and fermentation pierced the back of Walken's nose. The ground below her was littered with cups, bowls, plates, knives, forks, containers, washing machines, diapers and a feast of food scraps—half chewed and discarded.

The large grey blocks reached high into the sky. They had no windows on their side, with only a metal roller door on one face. Their chimneys bellowed smoke that was not from burning wood. Walken had never smelt this before. It was a thick black smoke and the noise of the flames inside rattled the roller door.

The wisps finally caught up with Walken, breaking the sound barrier. Their beams of light shone bright tails as they hurried to catch up with her. They came to a synchronised and immediate halt. The mood was tense.

"Hey! You're on my side!" complained Wooyan.

"Am not!" laughed Nodjam.

"Shut up, it's no one's side. It's everyone's side," yelled Yoont.

There was a stillness for a moment as they enjoyed each other's company.

A thunder came bellowing from the distance as the eddies of the wisps finally caught up. Like a roaring jet engine, the sounds arrived with the wisps. The bickering of the wisps caught up with only minor lag.

"Ahhh!!!" yelled Nodjam, "I was sleeping!"

"Everyone's always sleeping!" said Mirda.

"Get out of my way!" added Kawa.

"Ouch! Quit bumpin' me!" piped in Viola.

"You're touching me! This is my side," demanded Yoorda.

"What are you even talking about?" screamed Mirda.

Walken paid them no mind. Instead her focus was again on the distance, in search of Bunyip. She saw more structures ahead. It was a stark contrast against the obliterated woodland. There were a few of them of different sizes. Their roofs were pointed and splotched with striped paperbark. Large panels of wood were crudely hinged on the opening of the structure. They hung askew and creaked against the force of the breeze.

Outside, on the street, clearings between the

buildings were splotched with muddy footprints.

He's close… she scowled in her mind.

There were red brick buildings along the side of the street in the middle of the camp, each two stories tall. One had on the front, in big stone markings, a capital S with two lines crossed through it vertically. Strong stone pillars stretched from the steps to the ceiling, holding up the tremendous weight of the structure.

The other had a logo above its door of an angled drafting compass atop a right-angled ruler. Its walls were solid concrete and a deep blue that fitted with its bleak surroundings. At the end of the street, on top of a small hill, was a huge manor that stood three stories above the rest. It rose high above the settlement and watched down from its perch. Three pillars stood out the front of its doors, holding up the sizeable overhanging balcony above.

The panel of the second storey window flung open like out of an old western. Bunyip popped his lumpy head out of the opening, his eyes lit up with the return of his friend.

"WALKEN! 'owthebloody'ellarya?" slurred Bunyip. "You're a bit far outta the bush, aren't ya?"

"What have you done with all the trees? I asked you not to clear anymore. Not to mention we can't get them to grow back! What have you done?!" huffed Walken. Her white core began to illuminate and fade in breathing rhythm with a lingering frustration that made her swell with rage.

"Never you moind. I've made it betta. It was too woody. Not enough room for moi buildings. Come inside, it's too hot. I've got the egg-nishener on."

"And the waterways? You've cut them off with that horrible thing in the middle."

"Oh, you mean the dam. I needed it though. For the hydroelectricity, you see. Awful hot here. Extremely uncomfortable. Borderline unnatural if you ask me."

"Hydroelectricity?"

"You got it. Power. For my aircon. Got it cranking in here. You wanna come in outta the elements?"

"No… not at all. What is that place? Back from the direction I came," asked Walken.

"Well, depends where you came from. I've got quite the territory you know."

"West."

"West, west, west… You mean my little community? Great isn't it. I'm pretty gracious aren't I, helpin' them like that."

"Gracious?! You've trapped them away in some broken down corner of your clearing!"

"I'm helping them," claimed Bunyip, closing his eyes with a stubborn smugness.

"But they have everything they need out there! You have to let their spirits cycle and let them be free."

"Ahh, bunch of hub-bubs. Trust me, them living there is a far more sensible way for them to live. Besides, it's far too hot and harsh out there. No one can survive on their own! They need me, you see."

"...I asked you not to clear anymore. We had an agreement and you went against your word."

"What agreement? Do you have that in writing? The agreement is that I am the most advanced, so I have taken it upon myself to help those around me."

"And how are you helping, exactly?"

"Elevation, you see. Getting them on my level. We can all be in this together once we all operate on the same principles. I'll treat them equally once they're a few generations into the system. Until then, we're still in transition."

"You what?! You're outnumbered hundreds of thousands to one in this land. And you suggest that you're the one who's miraculously figured it all out? The secrets of the world and the nature of truth?"

"You got it. Pretty cool, right? I'm great."

"Why wouldn't you think to assimilate yourself in the land around you?"

"Oh no… You've misunderstood, haha. I'll speak slower for you, it must be tough to keep up. I wouldn't live out there, HA! Can you imagine... But they love it. It's a lifestyle choice, you see. They're used to those conditions, you know?"

"You have the protectors of the river marooned in the desert away from their waterway. You have the caretakers of the forest confined to the sands. You have the expansive desert roamers confined to space with barely room to stretch out. What about this is helping, exactly?"

"Exactly. They're all the same, you know. No idea why they spread out so far. Come to think of it, it's strange they don't speak too much to each other, neither. Oh well. You see, they lack education. All these things around them that they never figured out. Now it's mine."

"What's yours?"

"All of it."

"No, what is 'yours'?"

"Look, I don't have time to rap semantics. I have the infrastructure to take proper care of them. They don't even have air-con! My environmental policy is fantastic and I firmly plan on looking into establishing an action committee within the foreseeable future to achieve our aim 'if you don't like it, lump it.'"

Walken stared into Bunyip's eyes with a stern hold. Her insides boiled and her breathing was heavily pitched. The white of her core bounced between the ends of her light's spectrum.

"Tell me, Bunyip. Why you want to… Why do you want to see my fire?"

"Haha, you don't have a bad bone in your body. You're too nice, it is."

I'll go see Crocodile. He'll have kept a close eye on Bunyip and his bullyin', she thought as she turned away from Bunyip's big building, flinging up a small dust storm around the manor.

"Well! Thanks for stopping by. Guess I'll see you next time!" yelled Bunyip from his window.

The distance between the trees was increasing along Andee's journey. His feet walked a well-trodden path that wore the traffic of a thousand travellers in its compressed soil. The track was wide and carpeted with a well-pressed layer of leaves, twigs and dung. It bore straight through the trees and flattened them beneath the trail.

Andee followed the cleared path along the trodden leaves. They were sapped of their natural crackle and instead squelched under the pressure of his step.

Planted along the side of the roads were vertical logs, each one pierced with three strands of wire, which connected them in a row.

"Moooooooo," said the cow from over the fence.

"What in the world are you…?" Andee asked the bovine.

"Mooooo?" replied the cow.

"Yes, yoooooou," assured Andee.

The cow stopped munching the wad of saliva

woven with grass. It flicked the flies away from its face with its ears and stared at Andee with a vacant look.

It then lowered its head and continued to graze.

Andee continued up the path along the fence line. The poles were brittle with white ants. They had frayed the logs to fragile struts, too weak to last against a strong breeze. The termites feasted on the buffet in front of them.

"Ouch!" blurted Andee, looking down at the sole of his foot.

Small caramel coloured spherical pebbles joined the mix of leaves and dung below. They were scattered at first, mostly squished into a drowning mass of mud and dirt. As Andee continued up the path, the stones dominated the covering of the way.

Beside the gravel road and beyond the wire fence was a woollen critter.

"Bahhh!"

"Wow! Look at you!" Andee replied.

He walked over to the fence and lent over to touch the soft wool that blanketed the animal. Without thought, and consumed by fear, the sheep sprang into the gap between the wire of the fence. It panicked and struggled against the threat it thought it saw in Andee and flailed madly about.

Andee took a step back and shielded himself from

a wild cloven hoof. The beast had become tangled around its neck in the wire fence.

"Stop! I'll help you get out," cried Andee and he took two steps towards the animal.

It continued to flail, still petrified at what Andee might do, tightening the grip of the wire around its neck. It crashed about. It kicked. It shook and rolled. But it could not get free.

"STOP! I can help you!" Andee implored the beast and bent down to help.

A hoof grazed his chest and scratched him under his clothing. Another kicked him in the leg in the panicked chaos. Andee fell back onto the ground and clutched his shin.

The sheep continued to struggle and tangle itself in the fence. It began to slow its kicking and could no longer turn within the tangled wire. It slipped a final breath and perished in the fence.

Andee stood, still holding his shin and, on one leg, hopped over to the sheep. He rubbed his leg shin up and down and placed it back on the ground, putting only a light amount of weight on it.

"Why didn't you let me help?" he said through a defeated sigh.

A flickering of light over the ridge in front of Andee caught his attention. He slowly made his way towards it along the gravel road. The small stones massaged his feet as he walked them now with accustomed step.

Over the ridge and down in the valley was a small, poorly built, stone house. From its chimney poured a soft white smoke which beautifully scented the surrounding area. There was a window in the side of the wall facing Andee, through which he could see a man busy about his chores.

Finally, I've found someone, he thought.

Making sure he was in clear view through the window, Andee propped his swag against the nearby tree and waited for his escort to arrive. He laid his small shield on the ground. Andee got the kindling in a bundle in the bowl of the curve. He placed the smooth pointed stick into the small notch in the shield's back and began to turn it quickly. The hot embers from the frictions touched the tinder and caught fire.

He let his eyes play in the stars while he listened to the wood crackle under the fire. A shooting star ripped across the sky and seemingly exploded into a thousand pieces. Some time passed, and Andee slipped into a bored sleep, tired of the extended wait.

A vicious barking woke him with a fright. It escaped

past the chomping slobbery jaws of the incoming kelpie, tied close on a short lead. Above the dog's head was a lantern with a flickering flame inside. It bounced furiously from side to side with the haste of its approach. The torch and hound came closer to reveal their master, the raggedy old farmer who Andee had seen through the window previously.

"Oi dere! Whatchadoin out 'ere, boy? Aint you know deres no foires out 'ere. Dis moi land, now geet da farq outta 'ere!"

"Kaya!" greeted Andee, unaware of what the man had said. "I'm from Karlaboodja, what place is this?"

The barking stopped at Andee's greeting. A shaggy mutt with black fur, sprinkled with strands of grey, stared back at Andee with mouth wide open in a dopey smile, his tail wagging with a welcoming excitement.

"'Dis moi place, boy. Now go on and get."

He interrupted himself with a ghastly cough. As it shook his frail frame, the weight of the lantern wore down the farmer's endurance, and his shotgun waved in Andee's direction. His skin was thin and pale. It looked as if moist tissue paper had fallen over a sack of meat, as though, if it tore, it would spill mince all over the ground.

The coughing continued to the point the farmer

had to put down his shotgun.

Andee quickly searched through his bag for a remedy for the man. He found some eucalyptus leaves and flowers from the yellow jam wattle. He crushed them in his hands and offered it to the farmer.

"OI!" *coughh cough* "Get back! That'll be self-defence! The law'll beliee me!" *coughh* The farmer quickly forced the shotgun against Andee's chest.

"Ok, ok, I'll just go." Andee raised his hands and dropped the aromatic remedy to the ground. It fell softly like a snowfall. He turned to collect his things, quickly sorting through his dilly bag.

Andee picked out a small gem and buried it shallow in the earth.

Watch over this man. He will need all the help he can get to survive, he said into the quartz.

Andee left the sickly-looking man and continued the path in the direction he was pointed. A warm glow rose from a spot on the horizon that caught his attention.

The gravel beneath his feet was now bonded with a thick set tar that paved the road ahead.

He came to a wooden shack, still within the confines of the grumpy man's fence. It was a collection of wood panels that looked as if they'd been stripped from a tree with unbridled rage. Their edges were rough and beaten. They were bound with rusted clouts and frayed leather to a rugged frame of erected wooden poles which stood bowed and wonky.

This will do for tonight. I need to sleep somewhere! Andee thought to himself.

He rolled out his swag under the cover of the rickety wooden shed and went to sleep the moment his head hit the ground.

———————

The next morning Andee woke with a fresh layer of mildew all around him. It chilled him awake with the early light of the day. The birds were chirping softly as they tuned in for the sunrise. Beautiful high-pitched melodies danced around the old wooden shed.

Andee stood up and rubbed his hands against his arms to dust off the chill. He ran on the spot and jumped high into the air, jolting his knees to his chest at his peak height. He tossed his arms from side to side, interlocked his fingers and stretched high into the fresh breeze.

Steady footsteps rustled the leaves carpeted on the ground. A sloppy pant accompanied the sounds.

The dog from the night before peeked its head

into the shed. It rumbled a ferocious snarl deep in its chest at the sight of Andee and twitched its upper lips to flash its teeth.

"Kaya, Kaya, Yubba," the words stuttered out of Andee's mouth.

The dog growled louder and barked once, loudly, into the shed.

"Now, why are you so angry? Does he mistreat you?" Andee asked.

Yubba licked his lips and stifled his growl.

"What is it, boy? I have done nothing wrong to you. Yet you think I am to be feared?"

The hound sat on the ground, continued to lick its lips and let out a body trembling yawn.

"It's not your fault. If all he spouts is fear, all you'll ever know is fear. Come here, boy. Good boy."

Yubba cautiously moved towards Andee. His head hung below his shoulders and it moved from side to side, assessing Andee with each step.

Andee reached out and offered the back of his hand to Yubba. The dog gave him a gentle bop with his snoot as the final test. And like that, a friendship was born. Yubba wagged his tail and buried his head in Andee's lap. Andee scratched his ears affection-ately.

"Good boy, there's a good boy," cooed Andee, reaching into his bag for some food for Yubba.

Shortly after, Andee packed up his swag and started on the path along the sealed road.

Yubba followed closely behind.

"Oh, you coming with me, little buddy?" asked Andee. "No worries. Promise we'll look out for each other?"

Andee and Yubba approached a strange lumpy building on the side of the road. Its red bricks were bound with a grainy, dull mortar. There was little movement in the early light and the pair ventured further into the strange place.

Moulded stone formed the street, curbsides and buildings all around them. Two strands of metal railing were embedded in the centre of the cleared pathway that mapped through the whole town.

"Look at that one!" gasped Andee in amazement.

Before them stood a double storey thick limestone brick building. The windows were intricately crafted in fabulous arches. Thick stone pillars were chiselled into the voids between each opening. Fantastic marble statues of men and women draped in gowns were positioned on the street facing walls. On top was a magnificent dome that looked like an entire building atop the already brooding structure.

clip, clop, clip, clop, clip, clop came the rhythm approaching from the street behind them.

woof woof woof woof!!!

"Steady, boy. It's alright." Andee turned to see a dual horse-drawn carriage pushing hard along the road. Their leather bondage rubbed against their short hair as they sweated under their breast collar harness.

"Move out the way, ya bloody scoundrel!" screamed the driver.

Andee leapt out of the way at the last possible second.

"Sorry 'bout that, I'm new here," Andee replied, fixing his clothes.

"Stay off to the side, where you belong…," demanded the driver without slowing the cart.

The horses left behind two large lumps of excrement. Its thick black mound steamed in the fresh morning. Immediately after, the wheels of the cart smooshed the remains into the road, releasing even more of an odour.

"Come on… let's get away from here," said Andee to Yubba.

The pair ventured further along the bitumen road. The shadows of the buildings were growing with the sunrise. It seemed that with each step they took the town came more alive to the day. A second chorus of birds had joined to compliment those who ushered in the first light. Together they called the sun from around the earth and it peeked over the dawn's horizon.

Andee could smell the ocean on the breeze. The tallest building of all dominated the sky. He and Yubba went to the base of the huge structure.

Its high reaching spires were atop four storeys of solid stone. The windows, with their high arches, looked as though they were melting down the side in the torturous heat. Patterns of sprawling trees were etched all over the face of the walls. The openings of the balconies were like ribs that appeared to breathe with the wind. On top of the highest points of the tower were lower case 't's that watched over the expanse of the entire town.

Andee's amazement was interrupted when he heard a trickling nearby. He walked around the corner of the building to find a man propped up with one hand against the wall, urinating against it. His black jacket slumped lazily over his body, covered in dirt and soot. He was not wearing shoes, which had caused the hems of his trousers to fray from being dragged on the ground.

The man looked up from himself with his eyes still half dazed with slumber. He blinked hard at Andee and jolted away from his urinal.

"Oi! You can't bloody be 'ere! Whatchadoin'?"

he exclaimed. The man's black shirt bore stains of fermented grape and his white neck collar hung askew from its hold. "Get away from 'ere. Your church is on the other side of town. Go on now, get."

He buttoned his pants and hurried back inside to his quarters.

"We're in a strange place, Yubba. We'd better go…," Andee suggested to Yubba.

The pair travelled out of the settlement and along the road that had led them to this strange place. Yubba quickly dashed off the path and disappeared over a grass crest surrounded by sprawling paperbark trees.

"Where you going, bud?" Andee called out, jogging to keep pace. "Wait up!"

Over the crest was a body of water that glistened clean and fresh under the sun's rays. Lily pads hung on the surface of the pool, with a delicate white flower atop. Long grass bordered the receding banks of the pond. It was hidden off the road and offered a soothing tranquillity Andee had missed these past seasons.

"Nice spot, Yubba. We'll set up here for now. Give us a hand getting some wood for a fire."

BARK!

"You're right. Kindling first."

CHAPTER 19

The trees on either side of the narrow bush road touched above to form a tunnel of green. They swayed in the soft breeze that pushed around the uncomfortable heat. There was no relief from its gust.

A rickety cart fumbled its way towards the town. The spokes of its wheels were patched with wooden splint, bound with thick iron nails and leather. It rocked like a dinghy in a wavy sea on its bowed axles. Glass jars of preserves clinked against one another in the back of the flatbed cart. Its canvas cover, presumably once white, now bore the yellow stain of the harsh southern sun.

The wheels groaned as they struggled to keep up with the pace of the giant horse that pulled them. The huge black horse looked as though he had the strength of five. Its harness was padded with soft wool and its mouth was free of bit or reins. He walked proudly with his head high above his shoulders, his lush grey mane sparkled in the light.

A young woman piloted the massive horse, while her elderly father sat in the shallow recess at the front of the cart. She wore trousers with suspenders and a tucked in off-white shirt, with the sleeves rolled up. Her hair was short under a crisp short brimmed leather akubra.

Her father was slumped just behind her, resting under his salt outlined, stained wide-brimmed hat. His grey beard propped it up from his mouth so he could breathe easily. His hands were crossed over the chest of his blue buttoned shirt, lazily pushed into his makeshift belt that bound his pants to his waist.

Three sheep trailed behind the cart, each tied to the same length of rope that was attached to the back. Their eyes were completely covered by their overgrown fleece. They looked like clouds that had grown hooves and ever-chewing snouts. They grazed and laid soft pebbles on their trail.

A herd of kangaroos were lazing in the tall grass near the billabong where Andee had set up camp. They lounged like Caesars in the sought-after shade. Their heads were held high, expecting to be fanned and fed. The white gum that shaded them began to groan, full of a healthy winter's rain. It swayed heavily in the breeze.

Crracck! One of its huge branches released

from the sturdy trunk. It plummeted towards the ground and obliterated the smaller branches it hit on the way down. The thunderous log hit the earth with full force.

The kangaroos shot up from their relaxation and pounced for the path away from alarm.

They sprang out from the bushes in front of the horse and rickety cart. They jumped over the cart with a single bound and continued towards safety. The horse reared on his hind legs and bolted up the path. The wagon rocked and bumped, waking the old man from his snooze.

"What the BLOODY HELL?!" he screamed.

"Wooo boy!! WOO, MAGIC!!" she screamed.

Bahh!! cried the sheep, being pulled quickly along by their bonds. *Bahh!!*

Down by the water, Yubba barked and ran for the gravel road. Andee heard the commotion from camp and raced towards it. He stood in the middle of the path and faced the oncoming stampede. A freight train of a horse galloped towards him without any intention of stopping.

"Look out!! Move out the way!!" she yelled at Andee.

He raised his right hand, with pinky and thumb extended outwards, and aimed directly into the creature's eyes.

The glass jars in the back of the cart were smashing as they flew about the cabin. The old man had been tossed and flipped like yesterday's breakfast. Only one sheep remained tied to the cart, bahhing for its life.

Andee looked fiercely at the approaching disaster, his hand held firmly outstretched. He kept his pinky and index fingers extended, his thumb latched his middle fingers. From his eyes glowed a brightness that pierced through the panicked rage of the galloping wrecking ball.

The horse slammed its hooves into the soil, pushing two great skid marks into the ground. The force compressed the cart from back to front. It shot in the air, nearly toppling over the horse, and crashed back to the ground. The dust settled around the now two-wheeled cart; the other two lay smashed beside the puffing horse.

"MAGIC! WHAT THE BLOODY HELL WAS THAT?" screamed the old man as he climbed down from the wonky frame.

"Leave him, Dad, he was just frightened," replied the girl, still frozen to her seat at the helm. She looked to Andee. "Oh, thank you, thank you! He's not normally like that. What did you do?!"

"I just asked him. Told him it's all ok. He really hates kangaroos, you know," Andee replied. "I'm from Karlaboodja, they call me Andee, where are you from?"

"I'm Eden. This is Foster, my dad. We're from here." she said softly, entranced by the remaining faint glow in Andee's eyes.

"Huh?" said Foster, breaking her out of her reverie.

"Nothing, Dad."

"Who're you then? Whatcha doin' out 'ere?" asked Foster. Yubba ran over to him and put his front paws against his thigh. "Allo, lad! What 'is name?"

"Heh," Andee said through a smile. "That's Yubba, my little buddy. I'm staying just over the hill there, by the trees over there, down by the water. I guess I'm here to stop runaway horses at the moment, haha. But other than that, I'm just waiting. And who's this beautiful creature?"

"He's beautiful! Aren't you bud? Who's a good boy?!"

"This is Magic," said Eden. The horse bowed its head and huffed through its nose. "I can't even pretend to control him. Can you imagine! He'd hurl me into the next century."

An exhausted sigh rang over their conversation that settled the adrenaline of the encounter.

baahhhh exhaled the lonely sheep still tied to the cart.

bahh said another, slowly trotting up the path to re-join its reduced flock.

"We've lost about three jars and two pots, Magic," said Foster from the back of the cart. "And I'll have you know, that one of them was those treats you like!"

Magic huffed out his nose, hung his head and shook it in devastation.

"Yeahh, so you think on that for a second," Foster continued.

Eden hopped down from the bench and inspected the two wheels that had fallen off the cart.

"Well, damn," she said. "I guess now I'll need to replace the stint, to repair my repairs. haha…"

Further down the path was a plank that had severed from the leper cart. Eden picked it up and placed one end against a small tree stump. She drove her foot through the board with a commanding force and snapped it in two with ease.

Foster tended to the stock in the cart and re-secured the sheep to the back. Eden repaired the wheels with what materials she had and made do enough to get them rolling again. Andee helped where he could, lifting the cart while Eden secured the wheels back on the axles.

"There," exhaled Eden, "that should do it for now. I appreciate your help, Andee. We'd better get going before the sun sets. Gets creepy out here after dark."

"Haha, yeah it does," Andee replied, unsure what

she meant. "Well, I'll see you around then. Say bye, Yubba."

BARK!

Andee waved them off as Magic effortlessly hauled them down the road. He returned to his camp and sat down to rest in the afternoon sun, whose beams were sifted through shadows of the trees, their heat warming them to the touch.

A single bubble rose from the billabong.

bulloupp

BARK, BARK, BARK!!!

The bubble broke the surface and spat ripples over the stagnant body. A single ray of light focused on the water. Its brightness grew as it expanded to cover the whole surface.

The ripples touched the shore and rebounded back towards their source. As they converged, another bubble kissed the surface.

bulloupp

Well. That doesn't look good, Andee thought to himself.

CHAPTER 20

The Wulgi were walking through time in the world above and around, looking for Bunyip.

sniff sniff "Do youse smell that?" asked Dom

"Smell what?" asked Kojak *sniff sniff* "oo, yes now I do. It smells delicious!"

"I think it's coming from over there, in the middle of the clearing of that forest." said Dom "pleassee, can we go look? I'm so hungry."

"You're always hungry…" said Koko.

"Ok, I guess we can ask. But don't forget why we've come here!" said Kenny

They slowed their pace as they approached the source of the smell. A soft grey smoke greeted them in the air. There were small crude buildings either side of the group made of poorly cut wood as they walked through the trail in-between. They were low buildings whose doorways were so small, you, no matter your stature, would have to duck to get through. All around them was a shoddily built

241

veranda that had rusted old nails sticking up from its uneven boards. The sun had bleached the wood and stripped it of its life.

"Over there!" said Dom.

In the distance was a barbeque pit, made with red bricks shaped like a large throne and a huge wrought-iron flat tray placed over the arm. Beneath this was a blazing pile of wood, its flames licked the black surface of the hot plate and sizzled the meat above. On top of the plate was a tremendous collection of meat; patties, sausages, steak, kebabs, the whole works. It was a mound large enough to feed an entire troop of people — all of it sizzling festively on the plate.

In front of the barbeque was Bunyip, sweating immensely under the harsh rays. He tightly compacted the ground that struggled to hold the weight of his body. His belly popped out under the red vest struggling to clasp itself on its golden buttons. Sweat poured from the thin strands of hair atop his head and rained down to stain his white collared shirt. In his left hand was a tin of beer. The condensation clung to it like a crisp rainforest dew and cut against the stagnant breeze. Bunyip's heavy breathing while he poked the meat and sipped his beer stretched his clothes to their limits. The stitching screamed with every inhale.

"Kaya! Who're you?!" said Dom "I'm Dom.

Welcome!"

"Argh! What, the, well I never, err" Bunyip huffed and gruffed in alarm. "Whaddaya doing sneaking up on someone like that?"

"Oh, our apologies. We forget how quiet we can be sometimes." said Kenny.

"Who are you?" asked Bunyip

"We're the Wulgi," said Koko.

"The wall guy?" replied Bunyip, looking them up and down. "You fellas came outta the bush I take it. Dressed in all those skins. That's a pretty headband you've got on there, boy. Anyway, my walls are fine. They're the highest and strongest ever, you know. Back into the bush with you then."

"What do you mean? Just like that? Aren't you going to offer us some of that feed?" asked Dom, concerned he was going to go longer without food.

"You mean this?" said Bunyip, pointing to the feast on the hot plate.

"Oh, geez, sorry fellas. I just don't have enough to spare. I think I've got something though. Never you worry. Ah, yeah! Here you can have this." Bunyip handed each of the Wulgi a stale and hard bun with some tomato sauce squirted on the inside. "Now run along boys. This dependency can't become a thing; now, you have to find your way in the new world."

"That's actually why we've come to talk to you," said Kojak. "We're not sure where you came from, but we do know that you missed out on some critical education of how we do things here to maintain harmony and love."

"You've caused quite an amount of damage already, Bunyip. But that's OK; you didn't know — you don't know. So, we're here to help you understand." clarified Kenny.

"But what about the food? Hey, fart-yip or whatever, don't you at least have anything to drink? How do you get your water?" asked Dom

"Water? Ha! Nah, I wash myself with that stuff. Here, taste this stuff, knocks the socks off of water." Bunyip poured a thick brown liquor into an unwashed grease-stained ball-glass sitting by the barbeque and handed it to Dom. Kenny quickly took it from his hand to try it first, cautious of the offering. Kenny took a sip.

The liquid burned his lips, mouth, and throat as he swallowed it. He breathed in quickly, the air rushed over the burn and deep into his lungs. With this breath, he yelled.

"Argh! This is poison!" Kenny threw it to the ground, smashing the glass. "We don't drink this! Are you trying to kill us?!"

Kenny coughed and groaned as he struggled against the burn of the drink.

"Hahaha, and that's not even the strong stuff! You little guys need to toughen up a bit," gloated Bunyip.

"Bunyip! What else have you built other than

what Walken created?" Demanded Koko interrupting the tense atmosphere surrounding them.

"Just a little dam. And a small camp off in the bush." He replied

"A small camp?" said Kojak.

"Yeah, don't worry about it. It's more of a wildlife reserve, technically."

"Why'd you say camp?" asked Kenny.

"Perhaps it's concentration." replied Bunyip.

"What?" said Kojak.

"My slip up. I said camp. I meant reserve — just a slip of concentration. You know, why all the questions? I didn't realise I even had to clear it with anyone."

"Well at least asking would have been nice. They were standing right there the whole time, but you looked straight passed them…" said Dom.

"Who was?" asked Bunyip

"The people!" said Kenny and Koko simultaneously.

"What people? Not to my definition."

The Wulgi paused for a moment, stunned in the responses of Bunyip and sought telepathic council.

"He's using the word to change the rules!" said Koko.

"It's amazing the games you can play when you write the rules." said Kenny, leering at Bunyip.

"We've got to help him through this," said

Kojak.

"OK, you weren't really a part of the plan from the beginning. But you're here now – so let me explain the things you missed before and how we maintain harmony here," said Koko to Bunyip.

"It's OK, it's not your fault, Bunyip," said Kenny. "We need to make sure you catch up on all the information you missed. About the seasons, climate, resources, and philosophy to maintain this wonderful balance and harmony."

"Don't worry – this isn't your fault. But you are responsible for changing it," said Dom with a full and toothy grin.

"We better start with the seasons. Let's see, where are we now?" said Koko. "That's it. We have Kamarbarang, Birak, Bunuru, Djeran, Makuru, and Djilba. But they're special – special to this area only."

"You see, Bunyip, there are many unique and diverse cultures here – and you're going to have to listen if you want to survive the long journey." said Kojak.

Bunyip began cleaning his nails by scraping them with the fingernails on his other hand. He poked the tip of his tongue out of his mouth and gently gnawed his teeth against their fleshy sponge as he focused in on the filth from his daily chores.

"There is an infinite wealth in the land, Bunyip,

and it must be treasured. The responsibility is on us to maintain it with care as if it were our own kin. It is us who have the burden of action to care for the environment and all things, both living and non-living." said Koko.

Bunyip looked up from his grooming and stared at the Wulgi.

"All finished? Yeah, yeah, that's all great. It sounds very interesting," said Bunyip, disinterestedly. "Look, wall-guys, I'm not sure what you're selling, but it sounds a bit heepy jeeby to me. I just think that I know what'll suit better, you know?"

"How does one sell the truth?" whispered Kojak to the other Wulgi.

"No no – it must be our fault. We're not explaining things clearly enough," said Dom.

"Yes, surely that's it. No one can be this stubborn." said Kenny

"We'll try again," said Koko, doubtful of its success.

"Alright fellas that's enough," interrupted Bunyip before they could try again. "Get off my property."

"Property?" said Koko.

"It's like ownership. Well… it is ownership." said Bunyip

They each stood with a squinted look of confusion for a moment.

"Of the land? What a bizarre concept." said Kojak. He looked to his cohorts. "This is much worse than we thought."

"But we're not done yet!" said Dom.

"Yeah yeah, I get it. Use less, so I can take more later. There's abundance in the land. And wealth. A whole lotta wealth you said….", said Bunyip, licking his lips for another sip of his cold beer.

The sun had painted the low cloud covering with a palette of purples and reds. The streets were calming to the evening as the rituals began to usher in the night. Brooms swept the dusty streets under the silence of the fatigued sweepers. Eden was packing down her stall in a surrendered routine that let her mind play free in the fields of imagination.

A man dressed in a baggy, worn out suit climbed the ladder at the base of the light pole on the street corner by the market stalls. His eyelids were heavy with the comfort of many afternoon whiskeys and he had the footing to match. In one hand he had a kerosene lantern, in the other, a box of matches. When he got to the top of the ladder, he hung the lantern on the side of the street lamp. He slid open the box of matches and looked down to pinch one from the bunch.

"Wooah, halp!" he yelled as the ladder slipped into a crack in the street. Matches rained down and scattered softly onto the pavement. The man hit the ground shortly after with a thunderous *Oooft*.

"Ahhhhhhh," he grumbled out of his bruised chest, reaching for the flask in his back pocket.

"Arhhhh-mmmm-rhhhhh," he mumbled, interrupting his own groan for a swig of the brown liquor.

Eden rushed over to the man, lying there at the base of the street lamp, the ladder resting on top of him.

"Are you ok?!" she asked, lifting the ladder off him.

"Mmmm. Fine I guess." He took another drink through his grumps and stood up clumsily as if he was falling in reverse. He looked up at the lamp, realising he had left his lantern next to the gas.

"Shi… I mean, sorry lady. Sugar…"

"Haha, I've heard worse, let me tell you."

The man quickly repositioned the ladder, making sure it had a steady base and raced up it to stop the imminent danger.

"Don't know what's takin' so long to get those bloody electrical lights to get goin'. Bloody hopeless they are, the government 'ere," the man ranted, gesturing with both hands.

Eden secured the base with her foot and held the ladder as he climbed.

"You best be gettin' on. Not normally safe out here once I've done my rounds," he shouted from atop the ladder.

"Oh, no, the troopers are out. I'll be fine."

"Mmm." *burp* "Still. I wouldn't trust a thirsty snake near a tall drink of water, like yourself." He climbed down from the ladder. "Cheers for your help, lass. See ya 'round lady."

The man picked up his ladder and moved his way down the street, taking another swig from his flask.

Eden finished packing away her stall under the dull light of the lamp. She put her things into a small rucksack and threw it over her shoulder. The journey home to Foster was not far and her empty stomach ensured her haste.

The bar was loud that evening as Eden passed its doors. Rabbled conversation echoed out of the brick walls accompanied by an abused acoustic guitar being strummed within an inch of its life. Eden hurried past the few frothy patrons that had spilled out onto the streets.

"Farq that, you woudn't step up to 'im in a millon yers," slurred one voice.

Eden looked up from her feet to see that it was three troopers. Their uniforms hung loosely from their sweat and dirt covered skin. The white collars of their shirts had stained yellow with the toxins that leaked out of them from their evening activities.

"Watch your bloody language, Hank. Z'eres lady present," said Seb, alerting the group to Eden's attempted stealth.

Hank pulled his blurred gaze towards her.

"Gawww, look at that one," he said. "No thanks love, I shouldn't have dessert this late—thank you, sweetie. Hahaha."

"Hahahhhhh," laughed along Seb and Jack, the other two hyenas.

Eden hurried her pace and resumed her sight back to the ground. She could smell the alcohol through their skin polluting the air upwind of her. The currents of the air shifted. They collided off to the side and swept in a tame willy-willy. It herded the loose leaves on the ground in order and moved them aside of its path, quickly vanishing behind a corner.

"'Ere now. Where ya goin? The night is still young," dribbled Hank, keeping up with her hurried pace. "I've seen you workin' the markets, ay. You've gotta be the hardest worker there. And if you're not, I'm sure you can make me the hardest worker here, no troubles. Heh."

"Piss off why don't you? Not with that peanut anyway," she snapped back.

"OoooOOoo, boys, she's got fire! And on such a chilled night I couldn't think of a more fitting treat."

"Leave me alone! Aren't you an officer?!"

"Only when I'm on duty, lovely. I'm on registered time off now. So, a free man in blue is all I am to you.

And we get so tired, we do, us three. Protecting you all. Without gratitude or affection. Appreciation. How's about just a little kiss on the cheek? As a thank you for the service."

"How's about a swift kick in the goolies and you never look at me again, even in your thoughts?"

"Come on now, love, just give 'im a little kiss," said Seb, now flanking her opposite Hank.

"Yeah go on. 'Ere, just a little one," sneered Jack, approaching from behind.

Eden ran down the street, away from the bar, and hid in an alley beside the church. As she crouched in the shadows of its thick walls, her chest rose and fell heavily with the adrenaline that coursed out of her stomach and through her veins.

Three pairs of heavy feet followed her tracks to the corner of the church.

"Where'd she go?" asked Seb.

"I dunno. Check over there, I'll go down here," instructed Hank.

He walked down the alley beside the church.

"Hellloooo. Lladdyyy. We're only playing around. We're not after anything, just some fun is all. You like fun, don't you?" Hank said into the darkness.

"Arghh!" Eden screamed when Hank came around the corner.

"There you are!" leered Hank through a predator's

smile.

Her scream called the other two back to the dark alley. Hank quickly lunged for her, covering her mouth.

"Now now, we're all friends here. There's no need to struggle. We're civil servants, you know. It's a lot easier if you just pay your dues. We're all in this together, you know."

The willy-willy stirred again close by. Two currents clashed together as the winds spun in fury. It came to rest at the corner of the church, crashing against the immovable wall.

The three men picked up Eden and threw her down on a loose pile of hay nearby. Hank undid his belt and held the buckle in one hand as the leather tail gently kissed the ground.

"There's no need to struggle, girl," mocked Hank, lifting the belt above his head and striking Eden across the body.

"OI WHATCHA DOIN' 'ERE?" yelled a voice from the street.

The men turned with a discovered jolt.

"Pull your head in, ya peanut. It's way past your curfew!" snapped Jack.

"Get outta here, boy. Before you get hurt," said Seb.

Hank stood there, still with belt in hand, panting.

"Whooah. I'd be more worried about your breath. I can smell it from here. You must eat shit for breakfast, to talk it so much over lunch and dinner," replied Andee, taking a few steps towards the trio, "I've come looking for my friend." He turned to look at the girl. "Come, Eden. We'll get you home safe."

"Like hell you will! You're a smart-mouthed bushman aren't ya?" Hank raised his labour-hardened hand to strike Andee.

Andee's eyes shone an intense beam out into the alley. It penetrated the darkness and blinded the trio. They recoiled and shielded their eyes from the light. In that moment, Andee had frozen the setting around them. He moved around the men, Hank still there with his hand raised above his shoulder, the other two shielding their eyes from the light. Andee touched Eden on the shoulder as she lay in the pile of hay.

"No! ANDEE! They'll kill you!" Her screams continued as she joined Andee in the timeless space. "What… what's going on?" she inspected her perpetrators, now fleshy mannequins.

"It's ok now. We can go whenever you're ready," said Andee, reassuring Eden that it was all over.

Eden stood and, in a huff, brushed off the grass seeds that clung to her clothing. Her anger grew with each swipe at the pesky hay.

As they were leaving, she spat in Seb's face. Then she clawed at Jack's face, still grimacing from the blinding light. Finally, she turned to face Hank.

"YOU SON OF A BITCH!" she screamed in Hank's frozen face. Eden raised her right leg behind her and kicked him in between the legs with the intention to send him into space.

"Let's go, Eden. They can't hurt you anymore," comforted Andee.

The pair walked slowly back to Eden and Foster's home just up the road. No words were said on their short journey.

"Thank you, Andee," Eden said softly on the threshold of her home.

"I'll see you soon, Eden," Andee replied and gently closed the door behind her.

Andee returned to the alley behind the church to the three frozen troopers. He walked up to Hank and stood toe-to-toe with him and looked deeply into his eyes.

"Tell me, Hank, would you fear yourself in a dark alley? If you could feel the things you've made others feel, would you wake up in the morning and continue to inflict them? I guess we will see."

A willy-willy built in the wind close-by and Andee disappeared into the night.

CHAPTER 21

Dawn broke the next morning on a hungover jailhouse. It rose early with a penetrating heat that wrung you out from the inside like a damp cloth. Seb dragged open his eyelids over the desert surface of his eyeballs. The whites of his eyes were red with despair and below them hung thick sacks of thin purple.

"Eeeuuurgh." The noise ran over his parched tongue. "Wwwatterrrr."

Jack was slumped unconscious in a chair in the corner of the office. He had dribbled down his shirt, forming a yellowed, stained patch over his collar. A fume of alcohol wafted from him and polluted the surrounding area. As Seb walked past to the sink, he let out a deathly fart that rattled his senses.

"I'm never drinking again," moaned Seb with a defeated sigh. He held his breath and continued on to the taps.

The door burst open with a firm kick. It was the boss. His huge rounded silhouette stood poised in the doorway with the intense sun on his back. The noise startled Jack awake and a sudden gasp slipped from a pool of saliva in his mouth.

Couughh, coooough, cough, couug Jack heaved for his breath.

"Mornin' boss," yelled Seb over the room, sculling back his third glass of water.

coughh, coughh continued Jack.

"He alright?" shouted Capt. Wilmore back to Seb.

"Huh?" Seb replied.

"I said, he alright?"

"Who?"

coughh couuugh, cough coug

"Jack." Wilmore turned to Jack, "Mate, you alright?"

Seb walked through to investigate the commotion.

"Geezus, Jack. You alright mate?"

couu, cough coughh, coughh, cough, cough

"Ahem, ah-ha," replied Jack. "You bastards! I coulda died! Get me some bloody water, Seb."

Jack snatched the glass out of Seb's hand and sipped at it frantically. He took tiny slurps, rinsed them around his mouth and swallowed them.

"You could have died? Jack, am I to believe that I'm employing someone that almost died on his own spit?" asked Capt. Wilmore.

The room paused for a moment on the unsure edge between answering or surrendering to a rhetorical silence.

"You both look like absolute shit. What did you do last night?" continued Capt. Wilmore while he prepared his desk for the day.

"Pub," replied Jack with a mumbled immediacy.

"I've been to the pub before. I don't remember coming out looking like I'd been passed out the back end of a rhinoceros. So, what'd you do? Go on safari?"

"We had a bit of a tumble with some native in town," said Seb. "Real strange fella."

"What's a native doing in town? Doesn't he know about curfew? That's illegal."

"I don't think he knew," replied Seb.

"Tell him about the glowing," said Jack.

"Glowing?" asked Wilmore.

"What do you mean, glowing, Jack?" asked Seb.

"The guy. He was glowing as bright as anything! You didn't see that? His eyes were like lanterns, only brighter. I've seen those electric lights out in Launceston. Brighter than them even!"

"How'd you let him get away?" probed Wilmore.

"He tricked us pretty good," added Jack.

"Shut up!" interjected Seb. "He was tricky. He got around us somehow. All at once. And messed with our pants. He even tied Hank's shoes together! Fell right on his face when we went after him."

"Haha, that's right," laughed Jack, "drunk as."

"Shut it!" commanded Wilmore, wiping the sweat from his brow with an unwashed hanky. "Seb, tell me everything about the savage."

"I dunno. Wasn't very tall. Kinda matted hair. Fit bloke. I dunno mate, they all seem the same anyway."

"You said he vanished?" interrupted Wilmore.

"He disappeared, yeah, like around a corner. I'm pretty sure the little tike is just way quicker than us blokes."

"And he glew!" claimed Jack.

"He glew? You mean glowed, you idiot, and no, he didn't. Not that I saw, anyway, boss," replied Seb.

"Enough with your hallucinations, Jack!" shouted Wilmore. "Make yourself useful and go get my boy Hank, the lazy bastard."

"Fine," affirmed Jack as he walked out in a grump, mumbling to himself as he left. "Wish I was the bosses' son, get to sleep in and…"

Wilmore shuffled his blubbery mass towards Seb. He huffed and groaned and slumped himself in the chair next to him.

"Now," he said through panting breath, "tell me more about him. What type of things did he carry? Any markings?"

"Didn't carry much really." Seb moved his head around the room, tracing his memory of the event. "He had one of those stick things on his belt. A light jacket thingy. And some cuts all up his skin. Oh, and a small pouch that jangled as he walked."

"What did it sound like?"

"Kinda dull. Not like a coin purse. Not sure what was in it though."

Wilmore leant back in the strained chair and placed his index fingers in a steeple on the bridge of his nose, leaving his thumbs to catch his chin. He paused for a moment before continuing his inquiry.

"And you said he 'messed with your pants'? What in God's name does that mean…?" he asked from his reclined position.

"I'm not sure how he did it. But he filled our pockets with… he filled our pockets with shit. No one saw him tie Hank's shoes together. And, all in an instant, he fell to the ground like he took a kick from a horse to the goolies." Seb clicked his fingers, "Bam, just like that."

Wilmore leaned back in his chair. It screamed at its joints under the tremendous force of the moving weight.

"They're tricky, you know. Just think. They've got to out-number us. All this country. A thousand to one I'd say. We can't count them, obviously, but they're out there. And worse yet, they're stronger, smarter to the landscape. They have powers too."

"Powers?"

"Yeah. In their gems. These stones they carry. Like, unlock powers. So, I've heard." Wilmore stared at the ground in a trance. "Imagine that. I get my hands on their relics. Learn their powers. I could usher them into progress. I could bring them into a new age!"

Wilmore's face was wide-eyed and fixated on the ground in front of him.

"They would write songs about me. My name etched in history as the ultimate protector of the underprivileged, a moulder of raw material," he smacked his lips together. "Imagine if I had that power."

"Yeah, we could do some great things," added Seb, looking to still be involved in the dream.

A steady beat approached them from outside. Heavy footsteps ran up the wooden steps and over the creaking floorboards. The doors flung open and smashed into the walls on either side.

"He's fuckin' dead!" yelled Jack over the entire jailhouse. "Dead as a door post. All crinkled up like. Come on and look for yourselves."

"Crikey!" Seb shot up from his seat and fastened his pants. He frantically tucked in his shirt the best he could, picked up his rifle and hat, and made for

Hank's place.

Wilmore rocked himself back and forth to get the momentum to stand. His feet hit the ground hard and his body stood up.

"Right! Let's go!" he commanded his troopers, already out the door and down the road.

They arrived at Hank's house. The door was still wide open from Jack's quick exit.

"He's in the bedroom," trembled Jack skittishly.

Seb and Wilmore ventured deeper into the home, following the stench towards the bedroom. They peered around the doorway to reveal a crunched and contorted figure.

Hank's body lay in his bed stiff as concrete. His skin was yellowed all over, his eyes bloodshot red and two streams of crusted blood leaked from his nostrils. Hank's fingers were brittle and rigid, curled in towards his palm. The bed sheets were soaked in sweat and the blankets were thrown all over the floor.

Seb gagged at the smell and quickly ran back down the hallway and out the front door. Wilmore, of stronger stomach, approached Hank's body with his hankerchief as a mask to cover the smell. He looked over his pale skin. Its surface was thin and transparent to reveal the blackened veins of his body.

Wilmore huffed and hummed. Then quickly turned and went out the front.

"He's been poisoned!" concluded Wilmore. "There's no doubt about it. Jack, pick yourself up and pack the horses. Pack double the ammo as the last run, twice the amount of rope and triple the amount of powder. These brutal attacks need to be met with full force."

"Where are we going, boss?" asked Seb.

"I bet it was that bloke you said. You said he had markings, right? Little cuts? There's a tribe down by the big river to the south that keep giving us trouble. Stealing food and what not. I bet you anything he's from there. Sent in as some type of assassin, I bet. Well, let's send them our reply."

CHAPTER 22

"This is getting a little out of control now. We should stop this here and start again," insisted Kenny. "They've trapped the word and are using it against the world."

"They aren't very nice, are they?" observed Dom.

"No, not very nice at all," replied Koko.

"Why aren't they nice?" asked Kojak to the group.

"I'm not sure why they're not nice, Kojak," consoled Kenny.

"Do you suppose they've ever met Walken?" queried Dom.

"No, I don't suppose they have met Walken," replied Koko.

"Huh. Well, that's a pity," said Dom. "Have they tried looking for her?"

"No, I wouldn't say they have, young one," comforted Koko.

"No, no, no, there is not much to be positive about down there, is there?" said Kojak.

The Wulgi continued their walk as they digested

their observations. The silence was interrupted with an emphatic jolt.

"Oh, look at that man's moustache! That's the greatest thing I've ever seen. I wonder if you can hang things from it… I wonder… I wonder if I could hang from it… whoaaa," elated Dom.

A group of five men gathered in a carpeted concrete room below, with a bumpy popcorn ceiling and decorated hardwood high trestle beams. They all looked relatively the same, with their skin and bone bodies under their pressed suits, open collars and balding heads—except for one. He lumped his own excess in his chair; it pushed and bulged his confined shirt. Big yellow patches of sweat stained under his arms. Atop his lip and brow were consistent beads of moisture, although it was not that hot for the climate. His breathing was heavy as he huffed through attempts at conversation.

"I've read they're dying out, the poor things. They're just not suited for the landscape is all," reported Luke.

"What obligation do we have here? We can't possible offer support to all of them. That's just unreasonable on our resources," inquired Mark.

"Of course not. There has to be an in-between," stated Matthew.

"Why do we have to do anything at all? You've

seen their numbers are dying down. You see them drunk on their rum rations and whatever ale they can find. There's really no helping if they abuse what luxuries we already afford to them," retorted John.

"Well, we don't have to do anything. You're right there. But if we don't get involved, they'll be doomed. We've all read the accounts of them. Right from the first ship arrival. They've only gotten worse in their standing, you know. It's like we came at just the right time, in fact," replied Mark.

The room deliberated as each of the men mumbled their opinions to one another. They informally broke off into pairs and entertained each other's ideas. Neither of them listening, only thinking of what to say next.

"Well, the only conclusion I can see," Mark declared, capturing the attention of the room, "based on the evidence, is that the children would be better cared for under the state. Poor devils. You know, I heard the mother quickly forgets their young, sometimes resorting to eating them shortly after birth. So says Neville in his observations of them."

"You mean to take them away?" asked Peter.

"The race is going extinct; it'd be the only humane vine to offer in hopes of salvation. It's our duty as godly people to take them under our wing and maybe—over generations—they can be bred pure entirely," argued John.

"No, I understand that. Just the logistics sounds like a nightmare. I sure as hell don't want to oversee that," replied Peter.

"Well… me neither, now you mention it," added Matthew.

"Nah, I don't see it that way. It'll be fine. They don't mind being lumped together. Give 'em more friends to play and laugh with. They haven't got a care in the world, really," continued John.

***

"What did he just say?" questioned Koko, as he felt his blood pressure rise.

"What did he just say about the children?!" hissed Kenny, looking to Koko.

"They can't be serious… the children! Let me at him!!!" hollered Dom.

"Come on, we're going down there," ordered Kenny.

***

A stern incessant knocking at the door interrupted the meeting and rattled the walls.

"Get the door, will you? Tell them we're not expecting lunch for another hour," instructed Luke.

Matthew rose lazily from his uncomfortable chair and wobbled to the door. The cool brass chilled his palm as he gripped the handle and creaked open the door.

"Let me at him! I'll knock his stupid pointy moustache clean off!" yelled Dom before the door was even fully open.

"Stop pushing me! Hold him back!" protested Kenny to Dom and continued in his best accent, "why, yes, ah-hem, hello sir. We are here for the meeting of importance set for today."

Matthew stood in the way of the door open ajar, stunned at what stood before him. Four figures dressed in the finest kangaroo skin suits imaginable.

They had chosen to wear the same style of clothing as those they were visiting, only in their own materials, of course. A soft brown suede coated the well-pressed lapels of their three blazers. They each wore ties around the collar of their well-pressed shirts, so starched they couldn't move their arms. Their pants were a light knit hemp, the same colour as their jacket, that welcomed the cool breeze as it passed.

"It's… it's some of them here now," called Matthew back into the room.

"Whaddaya mean?" inquired John, taking off his spectacles and leaning forward into the desk.

"Yes, we're here for the meeting." Kenny pushed his way in past Matthew, stunned in his shoes. "We're here for the children."

"You're here to meet with us?" quizzed Mark,

confused.

"That's right!" affirmed Koko.

The room paused for a moment as the thought passed through the minds of the seated men. Mark chuckled, softly at first. Then John joined in and trailed into an uproarious laughter from the entire room. The entire room except the Wulgi.

"Whaddaya mean you here you meet with us?" asked Luke. "You can't do that, ha-ha, that's not how it works here."

"Well, we're here now, aren't we?" confronted Kojak. "So let's talk."

"Bad things will happen if you take those children, you know," warned Dom.

"Oh yeah? Like a curse? Some type of spell?" mocked John, "Aye? Ahh, I've read it all before. Ooga, booga! Haha."

"Please. Let's be serious here. You're talking about our children," pleaded Kenny.

"Just yours? Ooo, you've been a busy boy aye?" quipped Luke and his cohorts encouraged the antics with their blubbering laughter.

Kenny looked deeply into Luke's eyes. Luke's laughter slowly faded as he noticed a soft glint in Kenny's eye that grew brighter and brighter.

Enough. Kenny projected the words telepathically into their minds. **That is enough. Stop this immediately.**

The room bathed in a tense silence.

"We're here, now, to talk on behalf of our wellbeing," stated Kojak.

"Yes, well. Thank you for coming, but meetings of this level of sensitivity are private and are for elected members of the committee."

"And how can I run to be a part of this committee?" asked Kenny.

Again, confused by the concept, Matthew replied sheepishly… "You… you can't. It's not for you."

"I see," challenged Koko who turned to his colleagues. "Well, we're going to have to change that then, aren't we?"

"Come on. Let's go," said Kenny as they all turned to leave the room.

"I'm sorry you're making it this way," fumed Dom back to the seated men. "I don't like getting angry. And you're really making me angry…"

"Alright, on your way boys," commanded Mark to the group and then, turning to his associates, "Can we get some better security, so these types don't get in here when we're working problems out?"

"Beware the trader who offers a head for an eye."

The leather saddle groaned against the sweaty and uncomfortable horse. The ground radiated a violent heat as if it were just a single storey above the earth's core. The curved metal hammered into the horse's hoofs stretched and ached in the blistering heat. A silent pain unseen.

Jack and Seb lazily straddled their horses, slumped in a grime of three-day sweat and dirt. They travelled in the direction of the sunset in search of Andee and his tribe, assumed to be nearby. Two rifles clung to each saddle. They bounced wildly with each uneven step along the bush track. A jangle of brass and lead echoed from large leather pouches that offered a dark accompaniment to the symphonic melodies of the convoy.

"Hank was more the talker," shared Jack in the depth of the silence that travelled with them.

"I'll speak if you start, mate. I'm just a bit silent up here right now," replied Seb, pointing to his furrowed brow.

The dry dirt covering the ground scraped against the hot metal of the horseshoes. The parched scream of the earth like fingernails scraping at limestone. Jack leaned over on his horse.

"What'scar'non with boss?" he whispered to Seb. "He looks knackered."

Seb looked behind him to see the plump figure straddling his labouring horse, his face vacant of emotion.

"It's that story he heard. About the stone, or something. It's some type of relic, that, I dunno, makes him about to command? Or something? He heard it from some guy at the pub, probably some tale of the bush—but since then he can't stop talking about it. Just this morning, he explained to me, exactly the same as he did yesterday and the day before, about the supposed power of this gem. Like he had no memory at all," Seb explained.

"Well. Yes, sir, no sir, three bags full sir. Here we go. I bet I can get more bucks than you today," said Jack, playfully.

"Bet me what? You haven't got anything remotely appealing," replied Seb.

"If I get more bucks than you. You clear me bill at the pub."

"Well, now I'm not sure that even I have enough money for that."

"Aye. Cheeky bugger. So, whatcha say? Up for it?"

"What about the likely scenario of me killing more bucks. What do I get out of this deal?"

"I'll… I'll do your chores at the station for three days."

"Make it a week." Seb enjoyed the negotiation.

"Aww. Awwlroight. A week," finalised Jack.

The two men shook hands from horseback and the game was on.

"Are you excited to be an Australian?"

"And have a federal government? Ah, bunch of nonsense. Just another bloody group of people that've gathered together and convinced themselves they know what's best for everyone. Wasting all our hard-earned money. I've said it before and I'll say it again. Federation ain't nothing. Just a bloody fluffer word for fat men that sweat in suits." Jack began to breathe heavily and his voice shook to a mild rage.

"I thought you'd be for it."

"You're kidding?! My wife is dealing with hungry children, and I'm meant to give a damn about what we call this poor and dried up country? It don't make no difference what you call it. A turd's a turd," stated Jack from his soapbox saddle. "We're in hard times. And they spend all day talking about nonsense. It's why I'm out here. To make a decent coin and keep me family afloat. Keep me kids fed."

Capt. Wilmore moved slowly at the back. He made sure to be far enough away from the babble of the other two. He was draped with a faded red coat stained with crusted stains. Wilmore wore his wide-brimmed leather hat that could tell stories with its faded age. Two deep black eyes peered from below the shadow of its brim. His glance shook the air around him. The buttons of the jacket struggled to keep their grip against the weight of his stomach. A dirt sprinkled sweat covered his skin like a thin film.

The etched crinkles of his face and mournful valleys of his depressed brow stood out against his pale skin.

"How'd you end up here anyway?" asked Jack.

"Me? Well, I was stupid enough to steal wasn't I. Well, stupid enough to get caught at least. Apparently being hungry is a crime as well," Seb replied in a mocking tone. "I took a tall bottle of beer, some cured meats and bread for my mother at home. She was sick and… anyway. I had sold our cart but hadn't got the money yet, you see. So, when I went into the store, I bundled the items I wanted and I bolted. I had every intention of paying the bill once I had received my money, but no, that wasn't good enough. I was swept up, fourteen years old. Given a quick trial and a long boat ride. And wouldn't you know it, the last bloody boat of convicts they'd send to this dry and dusty island."

"I'm sorry to hear it," empathised Jack.

"Ahhh, it's not so bad. Back home I'm the lowest of the low. Really, I mean way far down. But here… ooh boy. They may as well call me the bush king! The only successful wrangler of this punishing wasteland and all its creatures! Ahhh, hahaha!" He laughed like a mad man.

The pair rode past an intricate marking etched into the bark of a tree beside the path. A beautiful combination of delicate dots and graceful outlines revealed a crocodile. Its body was wide and its tail wrapped around the tree all the way down to the roots.

"Here," commanded Wilmore from the back in a booming voice.

"What's that, Wilmore?" asked Seb, no longer interested in Jack.

"We're here. Dismount and load up. Be on the lookout for the sneaky bastards. They'll jump right out at ya."

The horses whinnied as they came to a halt. They scoffed their noses, stamped their hooves and shook their heads violently. Their brittle mains whipped their necks in distress. They've seen this mess before.

"Calm down!" Seb yanked on his lead and drove the bit into the horse's gums. "My God. You'll alert them all, you stupid beast."

Jack dismounted, unstrapped his rifle and began loading its six-round cartridges.

click

"You know I'm right, Seb," stated Jack, "these fellas can't sit 'ere and decide how we live!"

click

"Well, you aren't wrong," agreed Seb, loading his rifle, which was better than Jack's.

click

"The Yanks! Now they got it right. Declarin' the republic from the Brits. Arhh, but where would you even start with that," said Jack.

click

"A lot of gold in America, most of it in canvassed land too. Government is a bit lax out there. I hear they let you keep your find. Gotta deal with the competition though."

click

"How's that? Dealing with the competition?" asked Jack.

click

"It couldn't be that hard. I was in India once. That was hard."

click

"Tell me more 'bout this gold."

"This gold is gone already, riches beyond imagination. The Americans, Yanks as you said, swept it all up before it could be claimed. You could travel west here and search for that gold. Before the land is claimed."

click

Seb and Jack cocked their loaded rifles. They walked over to where Wilmore had been doing the same, only in a concentrated silence. He was the best hunter; meditative and calm.

"Alright boys. Let's move slowly, now. Wait for the bucks to move, then take your shot," instructed Wilmore.

"Aye, Boss," they replied in sync.

The trio moved through the bush with the subtlety of an elephant. Twigs cracked, leaves rustled in song, Wilmore breathed heavily and the horses continued to cry.

Delicate murmurs of conversation could be heard just beyond a border of short trees.

"Psst," Wilmore released from his pursed lips. He signalled that three were ahead and that the others should widen the distance between them for the attack.

They followed his orders and proceeded towards the noises in new formation. They bent their knees, numbed by the adrenaline, and kept their bodies low in the tall grass.

Willmore stood up and made a war-like cry. A pubescent squeal rang from his throat, as though as a mouse with his tail caught. Jack and Seb stood with immediacy and aimed their rifles.

Another human man looked back to the direction of Willmore's screech. In a jolt of defence, the man ran to his weapon that was propped up against a wooden stand. He quickly aimed towards Willmore and lunged to throw.

BANG

And Willmore shot the man. One of the others, who was two minutes prior conversing about the day's hunt, ran for his injured friend.

BANG

And Seb shot the man. "Gaww! Right in the head. See that?!"

The last of the three men ran for his weapon.

BANG

And Jack shot the man. "Ha! Never turn your back on an opponent!" he mocked.

"More coming in!" alerted Willmore. "They're armed! Take them out! Increase flank and pincer them as they push!"

BANG
BANG
BANG

"That's three, Jack! You're falling behind, chum!"
taunted Seb.

Jack saw a small group pushing back from the
west, out of sight to Willmore or Seb. He breathed
deeply and calmed his shaky hands.

He burst from behind his log cover and took aim.

***BANG, BANG, BANG, BANG, BANG, click,
click, click***

The white smoke from the onslaught of black powder
settled. A surrounding silence highlighted the ringing
in each of their ears from the gunshots. The smell of
gunpowder warming their insides.

"One, two… three. HA! I got 'em! That makes
four to me. Your clearin' my tab, boy! ha-ha!" gloated
Jack.

"There'll be more inside. Old ones still count you
know."

"Quiet you two. Clear the area," barked Willmore
in a war-like trance.

The three moved with caution past the fallen

battle lines of their unexpecting opponents. The silence was smashed with a crescendo of wailing, coming from down the hill where the other men had come from. They moved to the top of the incline and saw nine women of varied ages, three of them nursing young.

Willmore looked over them from above. One girl caught his eye. A tremendous beauty, he thought and did not break his glance for some time. She wore a gem that hung down to her sternum, the necklace shone into his ultimate desires. It made him warm in areas he had not felt in some time. He let his breath return to him, wiped the sweat from the forehead and walked back towards their attack.

"KILL THEM ALL," he ordered. "AND BRING ME THAT NECKLACE!"

"Aye sir," replied Seb.

"Whoa, what. Wait a second!" protested Jack. "Just the men. Now, that's the law. I ain't killing no kids."

"Are you kidding me? If one of these things gets away and tells a different group, they'll all be after our heads. This is the only way to prevent such savage retaliation from occurring!" yelled Seb.

"Jack, there is a story developing here. In our journey, we were ambushed. Two brave troopers, doing their colonial duty, acted in protection of their commanding officer, valiantly saving his life. I'd say that'd be worthy of a pay rise!"

Willmore cleared his throat, flung his arm over Jack's shoulder and said close to his ear, "Or, should this story need to be that in our conflict we were to have suffered the casualty of a trooper - leaving his wife penniless and, likely after a time, childless as well. But I could keep her warm for you. I'm sure she could keep me warm too."

A cold chill ran down Jack's spine. The putrid breath of unbrushed teeth and week-old meals invaded his nose and sat in his stomach. Blood rushed from his ears like a crashing tsunami.

Jack began to reload his rifle.

click

"There's a good boy," said Willmore.

click

Each delay saving a breath of one of the women or children.

click, cli...

BANG

Seb had already begun following orders.

BANG

BANG

BANG

BANG echoed into the eternal night.

CHAPTER 23

The salted winds of the coast by Bindjarra met Walken on her journey to Crocodile's home. They brought with them a calm that slowed her pace. It was a warm feeling that reminded her of home and offered a brief vacation in nostalgia. Anything was a welcome scent away from Bunyip's neighbouring dump.

The wisps orbited Walken as she travelled with a habitual routine. They did not speak or joke or sing, instead, they silently moved to the beat.

"CROCODILE!" Walken called out for her oldest friend. There was a mess of muddy footprints around the banks of the river beside Bindjarra.

The shallow waterways that moved through the area patterned the earth from the view above. Torn through the marshlands was a single trail of gnawn trees. To Walken, it looked as though a clumsy painter had smudged their brush along the other-wise perfect canvas.

Oh no… Walken thought to herself.

A single file of muddy footprints trailed off into the bush leading away from the heavily trodden path. The footprints plagued the ground. They pussed a toxic mud that smelled of death. Walken flew closer to the ground near Bindjarra's bora ring to inspect the scene.

Away from the clearing was a patch of destroyed bushes and trees. What type of dance is this? There is no order here, only chaos in the step, she thought.

As Walken continued along the beaten surrounding bush, she noticed a distinctive mark against a nearby tree trunk. Against the huge trunk of the wollemi pine was the ribbed imprint stamped firmly into the generations-old bark.

"CROCODILE?!" she called once more. "CROCodi—"

Walken lost all feeling. Crocodile's lifeless body was slumped over the central clearing, covered in mud and goop. His head was caved with repeated stomping blows.

The colour of the wisps faded in sickness. The white core of Walken dimmed. Each of the wisps turned their faces to Walken with a sombre gaze glued to the ground. One after the other, they retired into Walken's core and were absorbed into her. They turned away from Crocodile's body like a processional file, each of them dreading the events ahead.

The bright white core of Walken pulsated with a nuclear glow. Red filled her for a beat, and then orange burned its way through on the next, followed by yellow, green and blue. Walken hummed with a charge more powerful than the sun. The colours repeated, the beat slowly increasing its pace.

Kawa and Viola tended to Crocodile. Walken had not moved from the place of her realisation. They prepared his body for cremation and painted his coarse and weathered skin.

The stones of the ground began to vibrate in sync with Walken's pulse. After Viola and Kawa had tended to Crocodile, they faded their colours and joined the others. An intense beam of white light shot up to the sky from Walken and faded to reveal her final form. She wore a cloak of infinite colour and a fiery core that fuelled her rage. The beat of her pulse continued and was joined by a droning didgeridoo. It rolled its thick beat slowly over the air between the worlds. It resonated throughout and penetrated all that could hear.

Bunyip… Walken was filled with rage. Only rage.

CHAPTER 24

Blood stained the morning sunrise over the concrete settlement. Its people awoke the same as they did the day before and began their routines. The horses huffed and shook as they were dressed in their saddles for the work ahead. The streets started to hum with the building momentum of the day. Yet there was no mourning.

A weight rested on Andee's shoulders that had kept him up through the night. He had seen Tilda suspended in the sky, trapped in a world beyond escape, for her to inhabit for generations. An anticipation sat in his chest that fluttered his stomach. He was sombre in his contemplation that morning. Yubba looked up at him with concerned eyes and a lifeless tail. He walked over to Andee and gently licked his hanging hand.

"There's a good boy. Come on then. We'd better get it done," he said to Yubba.

Andee wandered himself into the town's centre

with Yubba. His head hung heavily with dread, and his skin was pale and thin. Wrinkled fleshbags sagged below his eyes from a disturbed rest. He slumped himself over a walking staff and slowly shuffled himself along the streets.

People stopped their conversations as they passed him. Andee's eyes still hummed a faint glow to the beat of the lingering drone. They looked at him with a perfect undertone of confusion and disgust. The women picked up the hems of their dresses and motioned them away from Andee when he got too close. Yubba jumped up on one of them and tried to give her a big, sloppy, kiss.

"EEII-ARGHHH," she screamed. "GET IT OFF ME, GET IT OFF, GETT ITT OFFFF!!"

"Haha, sorry about that, missus. Yubba just loves the perfume I guess, haha. Just wants a big 'ol kiss from ya. He's harmless," said Andee.

"Gah!" she scoffed in disgust. "My dress is ruined! I'm filing a report with the constables' department!" And off she went in a huff.

"Come on, bud. She's just down this way," Andee said to Yubba.

The settlement did not bear the same weight that had haunted Andee through the night. Instead, operations continued as normal. None more than the usual gentle hum of despair. It was a sombre place with little call for rejoice. Its people moved about their day, numb to the neighbouring pain and total devastation.

"Here we are, Yubba," Andee said to the dog as they arrived at Eden and Foster's unit. He bundled his hand into a nervous fist and knocked softly three times.

Foster opened the door slowly and peered out through the crack of sunlight.

"Who is it?!" he said with squinted vision. The metal chain bolt snapped loudly as it caught the door.

"It's Andee," he replied.

"Woof!" barked Yubba.

"And Yubba," added Andee.

The door slammed shut, it clicked and clacked, and opened wide.

"Oh yes, of course. Come in, come in. Would you like some water?" asked Foster.

"No, I'm OK," replied Andee.

"Not you," he said, filling a bowl of water from the tap and placing it on the ground. "There you go, lad. Drink up, hot one out today."

"How is she?" asked Andee.

"See for yourself. She's just through the hallway, on the left." Foster knelt down to Yubba, "I'll stay with this handsome fella. Who's a good boy???"

Meeeeeeeeeeee, Yubba thought, wagging his tail

with emphatic joy.

Andee wandered down the hallway. Its carpet smelt of damp dust. A type of smell that sits with the memory of a place. The ceiling was bumpy like popcorn glued together and painted over. He pushed open the door to her bedroom. It creaked on its hinges and trumpeted his entry into the room.

Eden was laying in bed, sitting up against the headboard. The left side of her face was bruised and swollen. Patches of purple blotched her face as the discolouration trickled through her veins. Her arms were scratched with small red marks that had dried since their carving.

"Hi, Andee," she whispered behind her injuries.

"Eden, are you getting enough rest?" he asked, taking slow, delicate, steps towards her bed. Andee felt the room was breakable. As if it was so fragile that a wrong step by him could bring the whole structure down, and with it, Eden and Foster.

"I am," she looked down at her feet under the blanket, "although I can't stop thinking about it."

"I've got something for you though. Something that you should have had all along."

Andee reached two fingers into his gem pouch and pulled out a large piece of quartz. It was smooth all around and, with its perfect transparency, appeared invisible at the right angle.

"Now," said Andee "whenever you feel unsafe, afraid or anxious, you need to look deeply into this sphere. Look deep and look for Foster. Look for the light of the future and all its wonders. Ignore the darkness and push beyond towards the light. In good time, it will all be as it should."

"It's beautiful, Andee." Eden stared at the gem for a moment. "Why're you telling me all this?"

"I'm not sure. But I guess I needed you to know. I think I'm going away for a while and I just wanted to make sure you were OK," Andee imparted with heavy heart.

"Where are you going?"

"Again, I'm not sure. But there's little I can do here to help." Andee rose from her bed. They shared in silence for a moment.

"Thank you, Andee. I really can't say that enough."

"I'm sorry, Eden. I'm sorry for the horribleness of it all," said Andee, halfway out of the door. "You're a good person, you don't deserve it. Don't stray from you."

Andee walked down the hallway where Foster was still playing with Yubba.

"Haha! He really loves these liver treats, doesn't he?!" observed Foster.

"Foster, you take care of her."

"Harder than it looks, but I'll do my best to keep up."

"Come on, boy. Let's go home." Andee slapped his thigh twice. Yubba shot up from the kitchen floor, licked Foster on the hand once more and joyously trotted out the door behind Andee.

Hot air assaulted Andee's entire body as they opened onto the street. He continued down the road towards his secluded camp.

Around the corner was Seb, on his way to the jailhouse for the first time. He saw Andee move in his peripherals and quickly shot his vision towards that direction as he disappeared behind a building.

Damn. Was that? No... we killed them all. Unless... nooo. Terror infected Seb's mind. He raced to catch up with Andee, now some distance down the street. Andee's curls bopped cheekily on his shoulders with every shuffled step. Seb dashed from building corner to horse cart to light pole like the Pink Panther.

Andee arrived at the road out of town and continued towards the billabong. Seb tripped while dashing for cover behind a tree behind the pair. Yubba stopped and turned back towards the town.

wooph, wooph, wooph, grrrrrr, bark, bark, bark!

"There there, Yubba. I know. I know. Let's see what he does," Andee said to Yubba.

Seb's chest beat heavily and he struggled to push beyond a shallow breath. He froze at the alerted barks of Yubba and caught his breath through shallow, desperate gasps.

"Leave it alone. Let's go! It's way better down by the water," called Andee from the peak of the hill near the billabong.

After the coast was clear, Seb raced back to town, thinking he'd not been seen. He held his hat to his head with his left hand and wildly flailed his right as he ran full speed down to the road. Coins fell from his pocket without second thought. His leather boots flopped about loosely on his feet as the dry dust beat them bare. Andee could hear him thump up the road from his camp at the water's edge.

Andee sat under the shade of the nearby tree. He was alone now. Alone without intruder. Alone with Yubba and the bubbling water.

A lone sheep wandered over from the other side. Its wool was torn in patches with a collection of dirt, leaves and sticks embedded deep within. Its mouth was cut and dried blood painted the front fleece in droplets. It cautiously ventured down the loose soil of the slope.

Andee watched the battered sheep gulp fresh mouthfuls from the waterhole. It closed its eyes with each sip. A return to grace it had not expected to feel again.

The water bubbled in front of the sheep, but it did not break from its obsession. It continued to slurp and suck at the disturbed rippling of the water. The bubbling pierced the surface once more and continued for an extended period.

The sheep jolted from its thirst and waddled around the shores of the water towards Andee.

"Ha. You're OK, fella," Andee said to the sheep as he waited by that billabong. The sheep looked back at Andee with its goggled eyes pointing dementedly in random directions.

Andee felt a gentle rumble tickle the back of his legs from the ground. He let crack a soft smile.

Here they come.

"You best be getting on there, Yubba. I'll see you soon. Go on to Foster, I think he has more of those treats for you!" Andee suggested excitedly.

Yubba's ears pricked up as he heard the special word, treat. He bolted down for the road back to the settlement and stopped himself on the embankment. Yubba turned to Andee, his tail dropped, realising he would not be following.

"Go on now. Love you, Yubba. Thank you for everything. I'll see you soon," Andee confirmed once more.

Yubba woofed, loud and proud, and jogged back into town.

The rumble grew in the earth with increased vibrance. It stopped just over the hill bordering the billabong.

"Right, load up. Make sure you're close. Let's get this bastard," whispered a faint voice. "Watch out for 'dem tricks though."

Three heads popped up over the crest of the border and over came the troopers; one, two, three. Wilmore led the charge, his gun held over his head like a Napoleonic portrait. Seb was close behind but without the energy to match. And Jack was last over the breach.

No invitation fire? Well, that's just rude... Andee thought

"Kaya!" Andee greeted them with a wave of his right palm.

"Look out!" Wilmore called out as Andee raised his hand and the three took cover behind their closest tree. "That could be a spell. Don't let him look directly into your eyes, fellas."

The light of his new necklace caught the sun as he took cover and shone it straight at Andee. His heart sank to his knees. He felt his stomach retreat into his spine and his breath take on the weight of a mountain.

"Whatcha doing here, boy?" shouted Seb from his cover. "You should be back with your mob."

"Me?" Andee shouted back.

"Yeah! You! No one else here, is there? … Wait, is there?" replied Seb, frantically checking over both shoulders.

"Oh, err, I guess I'm living here at the moment. It's OK though, spirits have welcomed me well into this place."

"Spirits? Whatcha on about, bushman?" asked Jack, timidly.

"The spirits that watch over this place. I've cleared it with them. It's all good."

"Enough of this voodoo." Wilmore stepped out from behind his tree, the butt of his rifle firmly pressed against his shoulder. He peered at Andee through the sights. Seb and Jack emerged from their cover too and followed suit.

"Now," Wilmore continued, "answer the man. Whatcha doin' 'ere? You hiding out after killing poor Hank? You bastard!"

"I've killed no man!" Andee refuted the accusation.

"That's BULL! I saw him, dead as. Poor bugger looked like he'd endured torture enough for three lifetimes. And I reckon it was your spells that done did it," yelled Seb, his voice quivering at the confrontation in the air.

"I'm sorry, to disappoint you, but I still have killed no man," assured Andee. He turned to Wilmore. "That's some necklace you have there. Perhaps I should be asking you these same questions. I have killed no man."

The necklace grew heavier around Wilmore's neck. Its increasing warmth rested on the skin of his chest.

"Arghh. You did," said Wilmore, lowering his rifle after struggling to hold it up for that long. He pointed at the lost sheep drinking by the billabong, "And you're also a thief!"

"Oh, I have been busy!" remarked Andee in a sarcasm known to the area. "This animal is just lost in a place that isn't his. When he's out here, covered in that thick jacket, struggling with the heat, and no idea how to survive—how is his plight my fault?"

"You did it mate. I can feel it," accused Wilmore from deep within his throat. "I don't trust not one of ya."

Andee shot Jack a piercing look. The brightness of his eyes, lost on the other two, shone strongly into Jack's being. He became captivated like a moth to the warm hum of the dull street lamp. All sound around them became muffled like a grenade had just gone off in Jack's brain.

"It's alright, Jack. But go forward into the

day with new mind, for you are the only one capable of change. I forgive you," Andee said to Jack telepathically over Wilmore's rant.

Tears welled up in Jack's eyes.

"… and for that reason, I find you guilty of stock theft and murder. You little bastard." Wilmore shifted his blubbery mass under his belt and raised his rifled back to his shoulder. Seb followed suit. Jack did not move.

"Troopers! Aim!" barked Wilmore and the two raised their guns.

Then so it is, thought Andee.

"FIRE!!" a glob of enraged saliva sprayed out over Wilmore's rifle, staining its wooden stock.

Time slowed as the troopers flinched their index fingers to pull the trigger. Andee swiftly threw a handful of dust on the nearby fire that puffed a bright flash all around. A thick white smoke plumed all around the area Andee had been standing in. The bullets raced through the smoke, leaving soft spirals from their penetration.

Andee watched a single bullet exit the barrel of Wilmore's rifle like a snail in a tunnel. The troopers heard a splash from beyond the clearing smoke.

"Keep going! The bastard!!! THE BASTARD!!!"

shouted Wilmore. "Shoot into the water!! Kill him!!"

The troopers fired everything they had, reloaded and fired it all again until they were out of bullets. Jack's gun, unknown to Wilmore and Seb, remained cold. Although he had raised and cocked his rifle to shoot, his finger stood strong against the action.

The smoke cleared and the offenders approached the shores of the watering hole. The soft ripples on the surface ran in all directions over the billabong. They moved wildly against their stagnant nature, shocked at the disturbance of the day.

"Do you see 'im?" asked Seb.

"Where is he?!" asked Jack, more amazed than fearful.

Thick bubbles rose to the surface of the water from the depths of the billabong.

bulloupp, bulloupp, bulloupp

They rang consistently.

bulloupp, bulloupp, bulloupp

The billabong began to sizzle like a boiling kettle. A drone began to roll out from the area. It was a deep note that shook the leaves in the trees. They clapped together at the show that was ahead. A gentle glow built under the water that illuminated bubbles as they rose.

The quartz necklace that hung around Wilmore's neck joined in the beat. It felt heavier than it had this morning. Its glow generated a warmth that, for the moment, continued unnoticed.

CHAPTER 25

The Wulgi were standing all around in a circle. Andee stood with them in the world above. Walken and her wisps circled them high in the air.

"I just don't see any other option," sighed Kenny.

"Neither do we," agreed Mirda.

"Let's get it done! They've gone too far and need to be stopped, NOW. Let me handle this, it'll all be over quickly," demanded Walken.

"Then what do we do? How can we stop it?" questioned Andee.

"You can't stop it, not now. Far too much momentum through time," said Koko. "We'll have to start again."

"Ahhh man, all the way from the beginning?" complained Dom, "but it took us so long to get here!"

"Yes, young one. All the way from the beginning, but a different beginning. You'll be older, wiser, stronger. With everything you've learned, we can pay closer attention to things," philosophised Kojak.

"Let's start with that dam over there," Andee pointed to Bunyip's strandlehold on the rivers and clapped his hands once. A huge crack fractured the face of the dam. He rubbed his palms over one another as if cleaning dirt from them and the structure began to crumble. Huge grey shards of stone plummeted to the ground. Water sprung free in laminar pillars like rays of sunshine breaking through thick clouds. As more shards fell the waterflow increased, eventually collapsing the entire centre wall of the dam. Water raged free into the valley below and quenched its long waiting thirst.

Walken flew with an incredible speed to the camp of tormented souls. She got higher in the air as she approached to look for the little girl she had seen. As she got closer to the camp she could see no one. The camp was empty. There was destruction in the centre of the rusted tin shacks. Bunyip's statue had been toppled and laid in a thick bed of mud. A large hole had been blown out the side of the boundry, with thousands of footprints leading into the horizon. Together, they had freed themselves from the inside.

"And those ugly buildings," Andee said back with the others. "They have to go as well."

Andee brushed them off of the landscape with a soft wave of his hand. Bunyip's courthouse fell to the ground and burst into a cascade of gravel. His mansion disappated into the wind like exhausted ash in a late evening fireplace. And his new education centre, where he washed the brains of those indivudals outside of his self-righteousness, imploded on itself.

"What about down there?" asked Koko

"Ooo, can I begin that one? I've got a lot to get off my chest," begged Dom.

"Ok, clever man. Why don't you lead us off?" encouraged Kenny.

The beat of the drone continued to roll on into the atmosphere. It built in frequency and ferocity, and spread like pins-and-needles through the ground. The earth all around began to tremor softly and rang like the springs on a taut snare drum, rattling against the surface.

Seb and Jack had taken station at the pub in town to debrief about their recent encounter. Their skin still bore a covering of black gunpowder from their folly shots. The dark brown jarrah floorboards creaked and groaned with the patrons above. The windows were dim and suffocated the natural light. Inside were a group of escapists and sad individuals retreating from their woes.

"I reckon he drowned," postulated Jack.

"No way he drowned. I hit that bastard square through his chest. I swear it! There was blood splattered all over the ground and into the water," boosted Seb, sipping from his pint. "I definitely shot him."

"How can you be sure?"

"I just did, alright? Believe me. Anyway. He's dead now, so it doesn't matter. I reckon I shot him though. The bush king strikes again! Ha-ha!"

Seb put his glass back on the bar and licked the froth from his lips. He cleared his throat and wiped his mouth with a napkin on the bar.

"It all catches up with you in the end, the poor bastard," he declared.

At that moment the surface of his beer began to ripple. Waves bounced up through the bottom of the glass and up to the top. Seb paused his conversation and fixated on the glass. After a short pause, the beat repeated and shook the drink.

"Did you see that?" asked Jack. "Your beer just shook. I dunno. Maybe I've had a few, ha-ha."

———

Wilmore sat at his desk in the jailhouse on the other side of town. In his palm was the quartz necklace. Its weight had doubled since Wilmore initially found it some weeks before. He brought it closer to his eye for inspection. Deep within the stone's core was a dim light. It flickered softly against the backdrop of his palm.

"What are you?" he asked the necklace in a breathy voice.

The light pulsated a faint beat. A warmth grew in the gem, but he paid it no mind.

All around the walls of the jailhouse were photo frames with newspaper headlines, personal photographs and noteworthy arrests. They each began to rattle against their hangings. At first, they merely tapped their frames gently against the walls without notice.

———

Along ways away, down by the rivers of Karlaboodja, were the trees that the Wanderers had planted all that time ago. Their trunks now stood tall and thick with healthy life. The long branches led to a fantastic collection of lush green leaves. A thin vein of light ran from the centre of the branches, through the twigs and beamed out of the leaves above.

Each tree beat a tremendous glow to the rhythm of the pulse. Their grouping amplified their illumination and hummed a warm light on the horizon.

———

Kulanda was cleaning fish at the base of the Katakonda waterfall. Its delicate trickle played its white noise while she tinkered at her task.

Splash! A heavy clump of water fell on the rocks.

Splash! Splash! Two more followed.

Splash! Splash! Splash! Splash!

She turned to investigate.

———

At the settlement, the ground rumbled with increased ferocity. The morning crowd at the general store looked at each other nervously.

"Did you feel that?" asked one.

"I think I might have…," confirmed another.

The shelves rattled the glass jars and shook the tinned food. The bread was thrown from the shelves and the glass cracked in the windows. Items began to shake from their position and crashed to the ground. Produce rained all over the floor.

The walls began to warp as if bending in the wind.

"Everyone out!" yelled the clerk. "Quickly now! Out! Out!"

Just as his foot left the shop, it all came crumbling to the ground.

The doctor's office followed suit. It was empty that morning and its destruction was immediate. It shook three times from side to side, like a violent sea smashing a raft. It disintegrated into the breeze.

The bubbles of the billabong popped with furious consistency. A drone joined them from below the depths of the water. Its sound jumped out as the bubbles popped into the world.

Dark clouds gathered above as they spiralled around the billabong. The earth rumbled and tickled the Richter. The leaves of the trees that bordered the hill fell from their twigs.

Thunder rolled in from the distance, closely followed by a violent light show of impulsive and unpredictable lightning.

A mass exodus of birds darkened the sky to the sounds of a thousand wings flapping in the calm before.

"You feel that?!" cried Jack to Seb. "Seriously this time. You have to have felt that?!"

"Yeah, I felt it. Just a tremor. Calm your farm," replied Seb.

"I dunno," Jack said nervously. "Sumthin's not roight."

The frames on the walls of the jailhouse now thumped a percussive symphony with the shaking of the earth. One fell from its hook and smashed on the ground. The frames threw themselves to their deaths.

Wilmore was transfixed on the transforming power in his grasp and did not recognise the smashing glass. The light from the gem now shone brighter than a street lamp, yet Wilmore still could not look away. He stared into it with slack-jawed amazement.

"Oh… oh, no," he said to the necklace.

A red circle was burning into Wilmore's hand. The smoke from his palm rose from behind the gem and touched his nostrils. His eyes opened wider with desire and the necklace burned brighter as he leaned in.

A tremendous flash burst from the stone and crashed over the jailhouse.

Wilmore dropped the necklace on the ground with a thud of a bomb the weight of a thousand dams crashing and breaking over the land. A crater the size of a saucepan was dented in the floor in front of Wilmore. The flash of light and ground-shaking thud broke him from his fixation.

"Nooo! NOOO!" he shouted in a panic as he looked around the room.

Its walls were melting around him. The frames continued to rain down from their hooks and scatter their glass over the ground. The mortar of the walls released the bricks from their grasp and let them fatally fall.

The ceiling turned to liquid and, in a single movement, crashed down on what had been the building's interior.

—————

Kulanda walked closer to the base of the waterfall. She put her ear against one of the large rocks that propped up the cliff. It whispered a furious crashing noise, like the breeze playing in the opening of an empty seashell.

Kulanda looked up the face of the cliff. A single sheet of water barged its way over the drop and blacked out the sun. She quickly dashed for the shore.

The water crashed over the river and flowed down towards the ocean. The waterfall flowed with its original glory.

—————

CRASSHHH!!! A deep trembling rang through the entire concrete town.

"I bloody told you it was something!" yelled Jack as he ran outside.

"Hold on!" yelled Seb, downing the rest of his drink in one gulp.

They ran into the street where they saw a plume of dust rising to the sky.

"It's the jailhouse!" said Jack.

"Captain!!!" screamed Seb, pushing past Jack to rush to the scene.

He pushed his way through the small crowd that had gathered.

"Wilmore!" he yelled. "Wilmore! Where are ya?!"

Seb pulled up a large wooden beam that topped the rubble. Underneath he found a limp hand with a red bloodied blister burned into its palm.

"Boss!" Seb screamed and frantically swept the rubble off his body.

Wilmore lay there, yellow and contorted. The veins of his eyes were a deep red. Seb looked over Wilmore's pale skin. Its surface was thin and transparent and revealed the blackened veins of his body.

Without a word, Jack ran down the street back to his house.

Seb stared at the ruins of his boss. His mouth was wide open and vacant of solution.

———

The sky had cleared of the dark clouds and a prevailing fresh blue painted above. The water of the billabong had calmed and the breeze rolled over the leaves. A magic pallet of colour opened itself over the landscape. Reds and greens and yellows and blues all played in the symphony of the surrounds.

A soft wind stroked ripples into that stagnant

pond and, with it, Andee's voice could be heard as you pass by that billabong.

"Who'll sing a wal sing, for Tilda and me?"

Glossary

1 HUMPY - A shelter made of natural material.
2 WARLITJ - An eaglehawk.
3 WOOMERA - Spear launcher.
4 BORA RING - Central clearing of a community
    used for ceremony.
5 DURDADYER - Animal skin leg coverings.
6 WILLY-WILLY - A small whirlwind.
7 CYCAD - A sedative when brewed into a tea.
8 KURULBRANG - Kangaroo paw
9 GUNYAH A temporary shelter.
10 KWENDA - The original name for Bandicoot.
11 CHITTY CHITTY - A willy-wag-tail.
12 LARAGIDI - A burial pole.
13 WOODINY - White ant, termite.
14 YONGA - Kangaroo.
15 WUNDA - A small wooden shield.
16 WADDY - A wooden club used as a weapon.